WHISKEY COBBLER

IT'S ALL IN THE WHISKEY BOOK 6

JEN TALTY

JUPITER PRESS

WHISKEY COBBLER

IT'S ALL IN THE WHISKEY BOOK 6

USA Today Bestselling Author
JEN TALTY

*Sign up for my Newsletter (https://dl.bookfunnel.com/
6atcf7g1be) where I often give away free books before
publication.*

*Join my private Facebook group (https://www.facebook.
com/groups/191706547909047/) where I post exclusive
excerpts and discuss all things murder and love!*

Never miss a new release. Follow me on
Amazon:amazon.com/author/jentalty
And on Bookbub: bookbub.com/authors/jen-talty

"*Deadly Secrets* is the best of romance and suspense in one hot read!" *NYT Bestselling Author Jennifer Probst*

"A charming setting and a steamy couple heat up the pages in a suspenseful story I couldn't put down!" *NY Times and USA today Bestselling Author Donna Grant*

"Jen Talty's books will grab your attention and pull you into a world of relatable characters, strong personalities, humor, and believable storylines. You'll laugh, you'll cry, and you'll rush to get the next book she releases!" Natalie Ann USA Today Bestselling Author

"I positively loved *In Two Weeks*, and highly recommend it. The writing is wonderful, the story is fantastic, and the characters will keep you coming back for more. I can't wait to get my hands on future installments of the NYS Troopers series." *Long and Short Reviews*

"*In Two Weeks* hooks the reader from page one. This is a fast paced story where the development of the romance grabs you emotionally and the suspense keeps you sitting on the edge of your chair. Great characters, great writing, and a believable plot that can be a warning to all of us." *Desiree Holt, USA Today Bestseller*

"*Dark Water* delivers an engaging portrait of wounded hearts as the memorable characters take you on a healing journey of love. A mysterious death brings danger and intrigue into the drama, while sultry passions brew into a believable plot that melts the reader's heart. Jen Talty pens an entertaining romance that grips the heart as the colorful and dangerous story unfolds into a chilling ending." *Night Owl Reviews*

"This is not the typical love story, nor is it the typical mystery. The characters are well rounded and interesting." *You Gotta Read Reviews*

"*Murder in Paradise Bay* is a fast-paced romantic thriller with plenty of twists and turns to keep you guessing until the end. You won't want to miss this one..." *USA Today* *bestselling author Janice Maynard*

Heather Cobbler has dedicated her life to the love and care of the horses at Whiskey Ranch. Having been born and raised on the land, her loyalty runs thick and deep. So, when horses start getting sick on her watch, Heather will stop at nothing to find out who is harming these glorious creatures and why.

Even if that means teaming up the veterinarian who has been hitting on her for nearly ten years and doesn't know how to take no for an answer.

Not much happened in the sleepy little town of Buhl, Idaho, and that's exactly why Detective Crew Irvin had moved there from the big city. So, when it appears a horse is murdered out on the Whiskey Ranch, Crew wants to wrap it up neatly and quickly.

That means slapping the cuffs on the super sexy ranch hand, Heather Cobbler.

Crew's detective skills might be rusty, but he doesn't have cobwebs for brains and Heather is about as guilty as the sky is pink.

Only he can't prove it without putting his heart on the line.

*H*eather Cobbler stepped out onto the back patio of Boone's Bar and Grill, grateful spring had finally arrived. May could be a tricky month in Buhl, Idaho, when it came to weather, but so far, the temperatures continued to remain unseasonably warm and dry. She removed her shawl as she raised up on tiptoe and peered over the crowd.

Nothing beat eating outside while the hot new sexy singer Boone had hired sang his country heart out.

"Over here." Zuri Marsh, Heather's best from high school, stood and waved from the corner table with a little more excitement than necessary. But that was Zuri. Happy-go-lucky and always had a smile on her face, no matter what. Zuri was the kind of person who could make Heather laugh when she really wanted to cry. Zuri had always been her biggest cheerleader and Heather appreciated the friendship, even though sometimes Zuri could be a bit much to take.

Heather scurried across the peanut shell-filled wood floor, dodging a couple of the gas heaters Boone had put out, knowing that within the next hour, the temps would drop below sixty and that was pushing outdoor dining, even for Idaho standards. She tossed her purse and shawl over the back of the chair and plopped herself down. "I hope you ordered me a happy hour drink." She glanced at her watch. "Because it's ending in five minutes."

"I ordered six drinks." Zuri tucked her bouncy red curls behind her ears and grinned. "I know how to take care of my girls."

"I'm shocked they let you do that without all of us here." Heather inhaled sharply, enjoying the mixed scents of sizzling meats, potatoes frying in grease, and hot chocolate melting over a decadent dessert. This establishment hadn't been much to talk about until Boone bought it a few years back; now, it was the hottest place in town.

"Boone showed me to the table," Zuri said.

"That explains it." Heather had gotten to known Boone pretty well since he'd fallen in love and subsequently married Paget, one of Heather's close friends and co-workers. At first, she figured Boone would end up going out of business, because it seemed like he gave away more food and drinks than he should, but it turns out all he did was make for a lot of happy customers who kept coming back and spending money in his establishment.

Brilliant.

"Where the hell is your sister? Didn't she come with you?"

Heather shook her head. "She didn't want to wait around for me to clean up, so she went home first. She should be here any minute."

The waitress brought over six glasses of red house wine and some chips and Boone's famous guacamole. She placed it on the center of the table along with three plates and a stack of napkins.

"I'm here. I'm here," Alyssa's voice shrieked from across the patio. "Don't start drinking without me." She raced through the crowd, nearly taking off a couple people's heads with her elbow. "What a day I had. I mean, I love my job. I love teaching preschool, and the kids on the ranch, they are amazing. But some days." With dramatic flair, she brushed her forehead as she sat down. "Holy little terrors. And Kitty Whiskey, she's the best boss ever and has the patience of a saint and I have no idea where I was going with that and you." She pointed at Heather. "I can't believe you didn't tell me that Hayden Fox was on Whiskey Ranch today." She took one of the glasses and raised it. "Cheers."

Leave it to her to come in like a wrecking ball, say a million things, and not let anyone respond to any of it, exhausting everyone at the table.

"Cheers," Heather said. "And I didn't tell you because you don't ever give anyone a chance to speak."

"I just did." Alyssa tilted her head and smiled.

As the youngest, Alyssa always said she had to speak loud and fast just to be heard.

Heather wholeheartedly disagreed with that statement. Her other two siblings, Joe and Reina, were both soft-spoken. Joe more than Reina. However, Alyssa was the baby, and she did often get the short end of the stick. That said, she also got away with murder.

"Now, spill the beans on what's going on with Hayden Fox. Because I can't believe she'd come back to the rodeo. She nearly died." Alyssa stuffed her face with a glop of guac.

Growing up, Heather and Alyssa were not all that close. It's only been in the last few years that they'd become friends, but the gossip aspect of Alyssa's personality really annoyed Heather to the point that sometimes she reverted back to being the mean older sister.

Heather swallowed her frustration. "I honestly don't know anything about it other than she had a meeting with Annette, Paget, Cheyenne, and JD."

"Sounds like she wants to make a comeback." Zuri groaned. "Fucking figures."

"What?" Alyssa asked.

But Heather didn't need to glance over her shoulder to know what had soured Zuri's mood.

"Jim Casey is here," Zuri said under her breath.

"Why is that a problem?" Alyssa asked.

"Because he was being super weird at work today. Not to mention he kept asking me if I was going to be seeing you here tonight. Are you ever going to tell him you're not interested?"

"He knows we're just friends." Heather rolled her eyes. "Good friends."

"Are you sure about that?" Zuri leaned forward and pursed her lips. "I still think something happened between the two of you."

"How many times do I have to tell you that he was there—"

Zuri waved her hand. "He was there that night. He stood by your side. Yeah. Yeah. Yeah. Blah. Blah. Blah. But you do know that everyone in this town thinks his ex left because of you."

"That's bullshit," Heather said, though Zuri wasn't wrong. She'd heard the gossip and sometimes she wished Jim would just open his big fucking mouth and tell everyone the truth. It wasn't that big of a deal. And it didn't have anything to do with him and no one would be judging him.

If anything, they'd be waving their fingers at her, considering the real reason Bethany left town.

But she'd made him a promise and she couldn't go back on her word.

"Besides, I don't give a shit what anyone thinks," Heather said.

Zuri fiddled with her wineglass. "It's obvious Jim really likes you and I couldn't lie to him. You know how I suck at that."

Heather laughed. "Thanks to you, I was grounded half of our high school career." She couldn't take it. Curiosity was going to get the better of her anyway, so she glanced over her shoulder.

Boone handed Jim and his buddies a couple of menus before turning and strolling in Heather's direction.

Jim smiled and waved.

She nodded. But thanks to her friend, she was all of a sudden, painfully aware of how Jim looked at her and it wasn't with an innocent gaze. No, there was a spark in his eye that needed to be hosed down with cold water. But she couldn't be rude. She had to deal with him on a regular basis at Whiskey Ranch.

"I swear to God, Jim is worse than when Steven wouldn't leave Paget alone." Zuri let out a long breath. "You really need to do something about him. He's like a dog in heat. Even if you can't see it. Everyone else can."

"Would you like me to say something to him?" Boone asked as he approached the table. "Has he been bothering you?"

"Not me," Zuri said. "But he's been hitting on Heather and our girl here often doesn't get it." Zuri waved her hand right over her head. "Sometimes I swear a man could run naked through the streets with a sign that says *I want to take Heather to bed* and Heather wouldn't know what it meant."

"Har har. You're so funny." Heather pursed her lips. "Jim and I are friends. Good friends. Men and women are allowed to be friends."

Alyssa shook her head. "You went out with that guy from the rodeo a few months ago and ever since, Jim has been all over you and you've done nothing to discourage him. If anything, you act like you enjoy the attention."

Boone laughed. "I used to tell Paget she wasn't firm enough with Steven. Of course, he's a controlling, power-hungry kind of guy. Your veterinarian has a God complex. My ex-wife was a lot like him. I suspect he'll move on as soon as someone better comes along."

"I don't know about that," Alyssa said. "He's had his sights set on my sister on and off for years. Except for when he almost married what's her name." Alyssa tapped her finger to her forehead. "What was her name?"

"Bethany Aries," Zuri said. "They were together for a year, and then she up and left a few weeks before their wedding day."

"Who's she?" Boone asked.

"She used to work at the animal hospital with me, but in the billing department. She left after they broke up and no one has heard from her since. No one knows what happened. Not even me." Zuri fluffed her wild hair. "Except Heather."

Heather closed her eyes and took in a deep breath, letting it out slowly, counting to ten. She blinked.

"I didn't know her well," Zuri continued, "but she seemed nice, and oddly, she was head over heels for Jim until one day she wasn't. And then she just left town."

"My guess is the slimeball cheated on her," Alyssa said. "She has family up in Boise, so I bet she went there."

"You sure do make a lot of assumptions," Boone said.

Alyssa shrugged. "I'm shocked Heather here hasn't put a sock in my mouth."

Heather laughed. "I'm pretty close and since Jim doesn't like to talk about it, we should respect his wishes. I mean, he is the one who got left behind." That wasn't entirely true since he was the one who called off the wedding, but he let everyone believe he was the one who got jilted, even though that's not what really happened.

"You could clear all this up and tell us what happened." Alyssa waved her hands.

"It's not my story to tell," Heather said. "And frankly, put yourself in Jim's shoes. Wouldn't you just want this whole thing to go away and move forward?"

Alyssa shook her head. "See. She defends him left and right, and yet, she says she doesn't like him."

"I like him. As a *friend*," Heather corrected. "He's just not boyfriend material."

"Then you need to tell him that," Zuri said. "He follows you around like a sick puppy and we're all tired of it."

"On that note, I'm heading home for the night, but I told your waitress to give you the friends and family discount. Make sure she does and don't be shy to ask if she forgets."

"Tell Paget that when I left, both Dixon and Izzy were doing better. But I'm going to go back to the ranch tonight and check on them and if they don't turn the corner, I'll have Jim come out in the morning." She glanced at Jim's table and wished she hadn't.

He tipped his glass in her direction and winked.

She tried not to make a face. She didn't want her sister and her friend to know they were right in their assessment. Jim had certainly turned it up and she needed to find a way to turn him down.

Without insulting him.

It wasn't that he was unattractive, because he was actually quite handsome. And he was a nice guy. Kind. Considerate. Although, he was a bit on the arrogant side and could be annoyingly chatty. Overall, Jim meant well.

He was just not the man for her.

She didn't think there was any man for her anymore. Not after what had happened. Her life choices had been taken away and she could live with it, but it wouldn't be fair to anyone else to give up having a family because she couldn't.

"I'll give her the message." Boone tapped the table. "She really appreciates all that you do. This pregnancy has been harder on her than she thought it would be, but I suspect it has more to do with still missing her dad."

Heather squeezed Boone's wrist. "She's super focused at work, but I keep telling her if she needs time, we got it covered. Annette tells her the same thing, but Paget won't take her up on it."

"I think work is good for her, but I don't want her to be home alone too much, which is why I try to get out of here at a reasonable hour so I can go rub her feet."

"We could all use a Boone," Zuri said, fanning her face. "Or how about your new singer? What's he like? Besides being superhot."

"He might be a little young for you," Boone said.

"What's young?" Alyssa said. "I'm barely over thirty by two years."

"He's barely twenty-six."

Heather laughed as her little sister scrunched her face.

"Yeah. That might not be old enough for me." Alyssa finished off the appetizer.

"You ladies have a nice evening." Boone disappeared out into the back parking lot.

"Paget is one lucky woman." Zuri raised her glass. "All I want to do is run my fingers through his long, wavy dark hair."

"Doesn't everyone?" Heather's jaw slacked open and her heart beat a little faster. "Here comes tall, dark, and aloof."

Detective Crew Irvin had joined the local police department about three months ago and so far, no one knew much about him except he came from Detroit, Michigan, where he'd been some hotshot cop until a murderer hit too close to home and he cracked.

At least that's what Alyssa had found out, only the details were more than fuzzy around the edges. All they really knew was that Crew had let a case get the better of him, and he blamed himself for the murder of more than one person.

Never a good place for a cop to be.

Crew lifted his Stetson, showing off a fresh buzz before making himself comfortable at a small table on the other side of the patio. He shoved his sunglasses on the top of his head and smiled at the waitress who handed him a menu.

Heather couldn't take her eyes off the sexy cop. The man had entered her dreams more times than she cared to admit even to herself. He generally kept to himself, not socializing with too many people, but he always showed up to every local gathering, hanging out in the background, while everyone talked about him as if he wasn't even in the room.

"Oh boy," Alyssa said. "You've got it bad."

"I do not." Heather's cheeks flushed. "And are you going to tell me you don't think Crew is about the hottest man in this place?"

"Oh, he's a looker alright, but so not my type." Alyssa pushed her empty wineglass aside. "I much prefer my men to have the ability to carry on a conversation over grunting."

Zuri laughed. "If the men you date can actually get in a word."

"Whatever," Alyssa said. "Are you saying you'd go out with Crew?"

"Absolutely not." Zuri shook her head. "I dated a cop once and it wasn't pleasant. The only man I'd ever date wearing a uniform would be a firefighter and I've got my sights set on Dooley. Now all I have to do is get him to notice me."

"Try wearing sexy clothes. That might help," Alyssa said.

Heather cringed, watching as Jim approached. Considering the conversation they'd just had about him, she didn't see how him joining would go over well.

"Hello, Zuri," Jim said. "Are you all having a nice night?"

"Hi, Jim." Zuri leaned back in her chair and folded her arms. "So far, so good."

Alyssa excused herself and made a beeline for the restroom. At least she knew she wouldn't be able to keep her big trap closed and exited before anything bad happened.

Jim turned his attention to Heather. "How are Izzy and Dixon doing?"

"When I left, a little better. I'm hoping it's a dietary issue, but I'm not sure."

"Would you like me to come out tomorrow?" Jim asked.

"If it's not too much trouble, that would be great."

"No problem," he said. "I was thinking maybe it would be fun if you ladies joined my buddies and me for dinner. Our treat."

She bit down on the inside of her cheek. Jim had always been there for her whenever she needed him, and the rift between him and Bethany hadn't been because of that. He'd loved Bethany with all his heart.

But Bethany loved someone else.

"Thanks. That's real nice of you, but I can't stay long. I want to get back to the ranch and check on the horses."

"Would you like me to join you?" Jim asked. "I don't mind."

She glanced at Zuri, who turned her head, hiding an *I told you so* smirk. "Thanks, but I've got it

14

covered," Heather said, wishing she understood men better. Shay used to tell her men hit on her all the time and it always went over her head. "If I need anything though, I've got your number."

"Perfect." Jim raised his hands. He had the nerve to pat her shoulder. "Maybe this weekend we can go out and have a drink. It's been a while since we've had one of our little chats. I'll be in touch." He turned and strolled away, not giving her a chance to say no. Which was always the way with him, now that she thought about it, and lately, he'd been turning up the charm. She thought it was because he was finally over Bethany.

And that was probably true, only she hadn't realized he'd set his sights on her.

"All right. I will admit, he might be seeing me as more than a friend right now," she said as her sister reappeared and took her seat.

"Might be," Alyssa said. "That man only has eyes for you, girl, and unless you want to break his poor little heart, like his ex, you better nip that in the bud now."

"I'll set the record straight tomorrow morning." Heather glanced over her shoulder, catching Crew's gaze.

He smiled.

Her heart lurched to her throat. "God, that man is

ridiculously sexy." He had that bad boy attraction mixed with a dash of sweetness that said he was probably a mama's boy when he was a young lad. He had everything a woman would want in a man, except he barely said two words and when anyone did get him talking, it wasn't ever anything personal.

He was the kind of man that women fantasized about opening their front door, saying hello, and then taking off all their clothes, not bothering to get his first name.

"Why don't you go over and say hello?" Zuri tossed a chip at Heather. "I'm sure he doesn't bite."

"I don't know about that. I heard he left Detroit because he fucked up big-time with the police department and was on forced administrative duty and at the time we hired him, he had been suspended and was on the verge of being fired." Alyssa arched a brow. "Steven told me that Crew applied for ten jobs with various police departments and ours was the only one that would hire him."

"Do you know why he couldn't get a job?" Heather shouldn't have asked the question in part because if Alyssa had heard anything on the subject, she'd repeat it. Even if it wasn't true.

Alyssa nodded wildly. "According to Steven, who is a reliable source, there was this big murder case and Crew botched it and it cost innocent lives. After that happened, Crew went crazy and they were going to can his ass."

"You didn't tell me that." Heather tossed a napkin at her sister.

"I just found out today when I ran into Steven earlier." Alyssa shrugged her shoulder. "And I don't think Steven meant for me to hear his conversation with some of the patrol officers."

"You're seriously going to get yourself in trouble." Heather shook her head. "That's rough, though." She was more intrigued by the man who barely said two words to anyone, but always seemed to be everywhere, than the gossip that surrounded him. Especially when it was her sister that dished it out.

Alyssa wasn't malicious with her need to talk about everyone and everything, nor did she go around spreading rumors. Well, she did, but only to Zuri, Heather, and their other sister, Reina.

However, one of these days, Alyssa was going to repeat something she shouldn't and the wrong person was going to overhear it and it was going to get her into a shit ton of trouble.

All that aside, if any of what Alyssa reported was true, Crew was a walking hot mess and keeping him in the fantasy zone would be the best bet.

"Why don't you take a picture. It might last

longer," Zuri said, handing Heather a napkin. "And wipe up the drool from your chin."

Heather cleared her throat, tearing her gaze from Crew. "Very funny," she said under her breath. "For the record, I wasn't staring."

"Oh, please." Alyssa laughed. "You should go say hello to him."

"I don't think so. I mean, every time I run into him and we talk, it's kind of weirdly awkward."

"Well, you can change that." Zuri stood. "And if you don't go over and make the first move, I'm going to go do it for you. It's certainly one way to kill two birds with one stone."

"Don't you dare." Heather's pulse raged out of control. Her cheeks flushed and all her erogenous zones lit up like the Fourth of July. "Besides, after what Alyssa just said, why would I want to get involved with someone like Crew? Sounds like he's got a shit ton of baggage that I don't need in my life."

"Because he's hot, sexy, and he's not Jim," Zuri said. "Go talk to him and maybe, just maybe, Jim will get the hint."

"I wouldn't use another person that way," Heather said, shaking her head and folding her arms. "Besides, Jim doesn't need me to clue him in. I will just tell him flat out I'm not interested next time I see him. As my friend, he'll understand." She took a strand of hair between her fingers and twiddled it. "And I still think you're wrong. Jim and I have shared heartache. We're just—"

"Friends," her sister and Zuri both said at the same time.

Zuri raised her hands. "I think you're using Jim to keep men away. You might not do it purposely, but you do it."

"That's bull." Only, that wasn't the first time she'd heard that. Shay had told her that the last time she ran into him. He even went as far as to say that she kept Jim around as a way to protect herself from the pains of the past.

That made her laugh because Shay never talked about what happened and he did use it to hide from the present.

"Okay. Then it's time to date the sexy cop." Her sister winked. "And I know you want to go over and say hello and ask him out to dinner."

"I bet she daydreams about it." Zuri fanned herself.

Heather knew her friend and her sister weren't going to drop this, and the reality was that Crew stirred things inside her that hadn't been turned up in years. "If I go over, will you drop it?" She flattened her hands on the table, preparing to stand. She sucked in a deep breath. It had been ten years since she allowed herself to step out of her comfort zone and feel anything but comfortably numb. She'd had boyfriends, but nothing exciting. No one she dated gave her that little shiver when she talked about them to her friends.

Although, she never expected them to. Her life had changed and even if she managed to let someone in, she'd never fall in love, get married, or have a family.

It was a life she wasn't cut out for and even when it was given to her, fate stepped in and took it away.

But Crew twisted her gut in ways she couldn't explain and that was an odd sensation, and while part of her wanted to squelch that feeling, a very real part of her wanted to explore it. She sensed he carried with him the same unsettled soul. Where everyone else saw a damaged man who appeared broken beyond repair, she saw someone with a common thread.

Of course, she had no idea what his history was or if he was simply an aloof man who didn't like people.

And that she could relate to as well.

"We sure will," her sister said.

"I'm going to hold you to it," Heather said.

2

_W_hen Crew Irvin moved to this sleepy little town in the middle of nowhere Idaho, he wanted two things.

To live where not much happened and to have a quiet life where no one knew about his past.

The only problem with small towns like Buhl was that everyone was up in their neighbor's business and Crew couldn't step outside his house without half the street looking in his direction and wondering if he was going to work, or something else.

However, playing the role of the elusive new detective worked for him. The townspeople kept their distance, giving him the space he desired. People might gossip about him behind his back, but they didn't know the whole story and that was fine.

He'd come to Buhl so he could heal just enough to function as a human being. So far, he'd achieved that. He woke up every day and while the first ten minutes were the worst and it took every ounce of energy he had to get out of bed and do the right thing.

He did it.

And he was able to do his job without going off the rails ten times a day. Of course, he thought about his wife and daughter every second of every day, but the mountains and vast open spaces had helped him train his mind to focus on their lives. Their happy moments.

Not their deaths that he'd caused.

Crew lifted his water glass and took a good chug. Boone's restaurant had become his go-to nightly dinner stop. Whether he ate inside or brought something home, it didn't matter. Boone had the best food in town. It wasn't anything fancy.

Just tasty.

And it wasn't his wife's home cooking.

He scanned the room. The corners of his mouth tipped upward. Whenever Heather Cobbler was in any room, it was icing on the cake. Prettiest girl in town with the sweetest smile. Definitely eye candy, and who didn't like gazing at gorgeous art?

He leaned back in his chair, mildly disgusted

with himself. Every time he saw Heather, he told himself it was okay for him to appreciate her natural beauty and what he knew had to be a kind soul. He reminded himself it was okay to look, but he'd never become entangled with a woman again.

At least not someone like Heather. No. Any female he'd spent time with since his wife had died hadn't even been a name. They'd been a body between the sheets.

Sure. That made him an asshole, but the women he met knew the score. He didn't make them any promises, and if they wanted anything other than a good time in the bedroom, they didn't have to enter.

Most never passed his test anyway, and whoever said a man had needs didn't understand those needs were only desires that a man could live without.

Especially when they'd had the best in the world.

And lost them.

His pulse kicked up a notch as Heather left her table and seemed to be headed in his direction.

But why?

His palms became sweaty and his pulse increased. He hadn't had this kind of reaction since he'd first met Darla back when he'd been sixteen years old. His heart swelled at the memory.

He swallowed his beating heart as Heather stood over his table. "Hello, Heather," he managed, trying to keep his cool exterior. He had a reputation to uphold. "How are you?"

"I'm doing okay." She twisted a piece of her long auburn hair between her fingers in what appeared to be a nervous habit.

He couldn't be sure, but part of his job was to read people and something was making her a tad squirrelly. He just hoped it wasn't him.

Or maybe it was a good idea if it was. The last thing he needed was to let his guard down because Heather was exactly the kind of woman he could fall for and his heart couldn't take it. Just thinking about it brought him closer to that dark place he nearly didn't come back from.

"Can I help you with something?" he asked.

"Actually, you can, but it's kind of weird and awkward and I hate asking."

He wiped his face with his napkin and tossed it on the table. "But you're going to anyway." He waved his hand out. "Have a seat." Oh. That he shouldn't have done.

Nervously, she glanced over her shoulder.

"Can I buy you a drink?" Oh, for fuck's sake. He should really learn to shut the fuck up. His mother used to call it his northern charm. Which was stupid because there was no such thing. "I'll even buy you and your friends a drink."

"That's not necessary." She joined him at the table with a perplexed look on her face. She glanced over her shoulder a couple of times.

He leaned forward. "Is there something wrong? Do you need my professional help?"

She let out a slight chuckle. "Not really."

He tilted his head. "You have my professional hackles up, but I'm also personally intrigued." That was an understatement.

"This is so embarrassing." She let out a long breath. "But I'm just going to be totally honest because it's only fair."

"All right." This should be interesting. He grabbed his water and took a long sip, wishing he wasn't on duty and could enjoy a cold one over this story. "Please. Go on."

"You're enjoying this a little too much."

He wiped a hand over his face, trying to cover his smile. "I'm curious as to what brought you to my table like a nervous cat because the few times we've crossed paths, you're always quite confident."

"I usually am, but this is an unusual circumstance and I'm about to put you in an awkward position."

"I doubt that," he said, waving the waitress over. "Could you please bring the lady a drink?"

She glanced up. "Oh. A glass of the house red is fine."

The waitress nodded and scurried away.

"You didn't have to do that," Heather said, going back to playing with her hair. "But thank you."

"My pleasure. Now tell me about this strange position you're putting me in."

"You know Doc James Casey, right?"

"I do." Crew nodded. "He takes care of my dogs."

"You seem like the big dog kind of person. What kind do you have?" Heather smiled that bright grin that made her eyes sparkle like the ocean dancing under the sun. It reminded him of a hot summer morning at the beach, just him, the water tickling his toes, and the salty air awakening his senses.

Christ. Crew needed to get a grip. Heather wasn't for him. No woman was for him. He couldn't ever be with someone he cared about again.

It would kill him.

"I have a couple of mutts, actually. They look like they could be maybe a Lab-shepherd mix, but not sure. However, you're changing the subject."

The waitress quietly and quickly set a glass of wine in front of Heather before taking off for a different table.

"He and I are friends, but as of late, he's been putting the pressure on. I didn't see it and my sister and my friend over there are pushing me to ask you out in order to get him off my back."

"I see."

"God, that sounded awful. I mean, I meant to ask you out, but I thought it only fair to tell you about Jim and...shit. I'm just making it worse. Now, I'm acting like my sister, Alyssa. Shit. I'm really sorry."

"Don't be. I'm flattered." He rested his elbows on the table. "But in order for something like that to really work, for him to really get the hint, we should probably go out on a proper date and not just have this one little drink where I'm on duty and I'm going to have to leave as soon as my check comes." Nothing like having diarrhea of the mouth. Hopefully, she'd turn him down, believing this would be enough.

Out of the corner of his eye, he saw Jim leave his group of friends and meander across the patio.

Not good.

"That's really sweet of you, but I'm not trying to make Jim jealous or anything. I can handle Jim. I mean, we're friends. Pretty good friends, actually. He's not a bad guy."

Why the hell was this woman rambling on about another man? "I'm confused. Do you like Jim and want to go out with him?"

"Oh God. No. I'm trying to keep my friends from coming over here, fixing us up, and telling Jim you and I are going out or something, making this even weirder." She smacked her palm against her forehead. "This is not going how I expected it to. I think a glass of wine before I had food wasn't a good idea."

"Relax," Crew said with a slight laugh. "I'd love to go out on a date, but I'd like to know if Jim is actually my competition."

"We're just friends," she said with a bright smile. "Please don't take this the wrong way, but I'm—"

"My, my," Jim said as he tapped his finger on the table. "Detective Irvin. How are you this evening? How are Duke and Daisy?"

"They're both doing well, thank you." Crew had seen Jim go chat up the girls about a half hour ago and now that Jim was standing at his table, Crew wondered what game Heather was really playing.

The make a man jealous game?

Or get rid of a man game?

Either way, he shouldn't be playing. Dating wasn't something he was prepared to bring back into his wheelhouse. Not even for Heather.

"I see you're wearing your badge and gun belt," Jim pointed out. "Does that mean you're on duty?"

"I'm on my dinner break." Crew didn't need to explain anything to Jim, especially since Crew didn't keep the same hours as a beat cop. Technically, he was the only detective on the payroll, so he was always on duty, but he currently was punching the clock. As in, he should probably be in uniform, but he'd gotten away with not wearing one since he rode into town and he hoped to keep it that way.

Jim held his hands up. "No judgment here. I was just hoping my taxpayer dollars weren't paying for a date or something."

Heather arched a brow and opened her mouth, but Crew cut her off.

"I was about to ask Heather here out to dinner, but you interrupted me," Crew said.

"Actually, you did ask. I just hadn't had the chance to accept." She smiled. "And I'd love to. How about Friday night?"

"I'm technically off tomorrow, so that works. As long as I don't get called in, we should be good." Crew nodded.

"Heather, can I speak to you for a moment?" Jim asked.

"Um, well, I was going to walk Crew to his car," Heather said.

"I'll wait," Jim said.

Crew stood, taking Heather by the hand. "Have a good night." He led her through the crowd, stopping at the bar and settling his bill before pushing open the front door. "Well, that was interesting."

"You don't have to take me out if you don't want to." She ran her hand through her hair.

"This is the last time I'm going to ask this. Did you want to go out with Jim?" Crew scratched his jaw. "I'm asking because now I'm really confused."

"So am I." She let out a long breath. "My sister and Zuri warned me that Jim wanted more, but I didn't see it and I don't want to use you."

He reached out and curled his fingers around her biceps. "Do you want to go out with me? Because I definitely want to go out with you. To be honest, I've thought about asking you out the last couple of times I've seen you, but I'm a bit of a loner for reasons we can talk about another time."

"So I've noticed." Heather leaned against his patrol car.

"You haven't answered my question."

"Yeah. I'd like to have dinner with you." She smiled.

"Good." He pulled out one of his cards. "This is my personal cell. Don't hesitate to call me. Day or night."

She took it between her fingertips.

"Why don't you text me now so I can put your number in my contacts, and I will text you with the details for our date." His heart pounded in his chest. He couldn't tell if he was nervous, or if it was something else.

No. He knew it wasn't guilt, only he wished it was because that would make it easier.

His mother told him a desire to start over would eventually kick in. That was unless he returned to the dark place and even he didn't want to go back to living with one foot in the grave. His precious Darla and sweet little Gypsy wouldn't appreciate that. He needed to at least do what they'd want him to do—expect him to do—and go about the business of living and doing the right thing.

He could do that in small-town Idaho.

"Why do you look like you really don't want to go out with me?" Crew took her hand and ran his thumb over the soft, tender skin of her wrist.

Her cheeks turned a pretty pink. "It's not that. I just don't have a lot of room in my life for dating and I feel weird about this. About how it all came about."

He leaned in and pressed his lips over hers in a gentle kiss. It was short, and not necessarily romantic, but he did let them linger more than a few seconds.

A slight moan tickled the back of her throat. Without thinking, she gripped his shoulders, leaning into his strong frame.

He wrapped his arms around her waist, pulling her close to his chest, keeping the kiss going. He tasted like strawberries dipped in chocolate milk.

His tongue twisted and twirled around hers in an exotic dance.

She blinked as he pulled back.

"That was unexpected," she whispered.

"I hadn't planned it," he admitted. "And I wouldn't mind doing it again, but I've got to get back to patrolling. I'm technically not on detective duty tonight and just a regular beat cop."

"What does that mean, exactly?"

"Three days a week, or whenever anyone takes a vacation day, I take their shifts. Otherwise, I'm on call for stolen bikes, missing cows, or my all-time favorite, the stolen Easter eggs turned vandalism on the car dealership."

Heather covered her lips and laughed. "You haven't been here during the missing pumpkins at Halloween. You'll love that."

"What is it with small towns?"

"It's mostly good fun," she said. "Every holiday certain people pick names out of a hat and we play pranks. Sometimes it gets out of hand. What you got caught up in with the egged cars was an old grudge and it will probably happen again on the Fourth of July."

"Good to know." He glanced over his shoulder. "I have to get going. I'll see you tomorrow, but call me if, well, if you feel like it."

"Thanks."

Crew jogged around the hood of his vehicle and climbed behind the steering wheel. He pulled down the visor and snagged the image of his late wife and daughter. He ran his finger over the picture. His little girl had just turned six when her life had been taken by a monster.

A deranged crazy killer that Crew had brought right to his front doorstep.

It didn't matter that he'd successfully brought a murderer to justice. It was a little too late. *His* wife and daughter had paid the ultimate price.

"I miss you both," he whispered. "I'm doing my best to make a life for myself here. I really am. I'm even going on a date." He rubbed his eye. Perhaps he should cancel. He couldn't give Heather any kind of real relationship. Hell, he probably couldn't even give her a good time.

He tucked the picture away and turned the engine on.

Darla would tell him to sleep on it, so that's exactly what he'd do.

3

"*H*ey, Izzy girl." Heather rubbed the horse's nose, but the poor thing couldn't even stand. "What's going on with you and Dixon?" She held out an apple slice, but Izzy turned her head. Setting it on the ground, she stood and stepped out of the stall. She glanced at her watch. Jim said he'd be by around five. It was now five-thirty, and Crew was supposed to be picking her up in an hour, but at this rate, she'd never make it back to her place, much less have time to take a quick shower and change.

"Why don't you leave. I know you've got plans," Cheyenne Whiskey said from behind her desk. "I can stay and deal with Jim."

"It's okay. Jim and I have been texting all day, and I kind of want to talk to him." Heather leaned against the doorjamb.

"About the horses?"

She shook her head. "Something personal."

Cheyenne set her pencil down and folded her hands, resting them on the desk. "I know I'm still a bit of the outsider on this ranch."

"I wouldn't say that." Heather had always felt a bit bad for Cheyenne for the way many treated her since her return to Whiskey Ranch.

"I appreciate that, but I do know what some people have said behind my back and I get it. I broke my husband's heart when I left, and then I kept his son from him for years."

"You had your reasons."

Cheyenne nodded. "Doesn't mean I was right in what I did." She held up her hand. "And just because JB and his family forgives me." She glanced down and patted her belly. "And we've all moved on. Doesn't mean that everyone else on this ranch respects me as JB's wife, especially when everyone thinks I'm a bit of a hard-ass."

Heather laughed. "I wouldn't go that far. I would say you speak your mind."

"Bingo." Cheyenne waggled her finger. "Which is why I'm going to stick my nose in where it doesn't belong where Jim is concerned. I might not know him like you do, but he's really got it bad for you."

"So I'm learning, which is why I want to talk to

him and I figure this would be the best environment to do it in."

"I have to agree." Cheyenne leaned back and rubbed her belly.

"How are you feeling?" Heather asked.

"Pregnant." Cheyenne laughed. "You should really be asking my husband that. He didn't get the privilege of being around me the last time and he's totally freaked out." She leaned back and patted her belly. "He felt the baby move this morning and then saw my stomach wiggle and it reminded him of an alien."

"I don't see JB being the squeamish type," Heather said.

"He's generally not. But between having to answer Jimmy's very specific questions about where babies come from, how they are born, and trying to make up for not being around the first time, he's got himself all worked up into a tizzy. Poor man." Cheyenne smiled. "I keep telling him to relax. That I'm fine and this is all normal as do all his family, but he's just turned into a pile of nervous cuteness."

"He is pretty adorable." Heather pulled out her cell and pulled up Crew's contact information.

Heather: *Stuck at the ranch waiting for Jim to come examine a couple of the horses. I don't know how long it's going to be.*

Bubbles popped up right away.

Crew: I'll meet you at the ranch.

Heather smiled.

"What has you all giddy and blushy?" Cheyenne asked.

"Things I shouldn't be thinking about, much less doing." Heather let out a puff of air as she took a seat. She stared at the screen before sending a quick response, agreeing to Crew's proposal.

"Does this have anything to do with a handsome detective?" Cheyenne asked.

Heather clutched her cell. Her heart pounded in her chest. Butterflies filled her gut as if she were twelve years old and attending her first school dance.

"Excuse me?"

"You forget Boone tells Paget everything and Paget tells me, and half the bar saw Crew kiss you last night."

"No." Heather's heart dropped like a ton of bricks to her gut. "You've got to be kidding me." The last thing she needed was to be the center of town gossip, especially with her family.

Once her mother caught wind of this, she'd be stopping by Crew's place with freshly baked cookies on a daily basis.

"I'm shocked no one has harassed you yet today," Cheyenne said. "I was told it was right in front of his patrol car, under the streetlight, and right on the lips." She raised her fingers to her mouth and made a smacking noise.

Heather groaned. "Wonderful. We're going out to dinner tonight."

"Oh, that's exciting." Cheyenne laced her fingers together, resting her hands on her stomach. "Really. You should leave. I can take care of things here and I'll even put the bug in Jim's ear. I'm sure he's heard about that kiss."

"Too late. Crew said he'd meet me here." Heather waved her phone. "What the hell am I going to do about Jim? I don't want to hurt his feelings."

Cheyenne narrowed her stare. "You have to be honest, or it's going to get worse, for him."

"I can't believe I let it get this out of control."

"Jim's pretty subtle in his attempts to get you to notice him." Cheyenne shrugged. "Don't worry too much about it. Jim's a big boy. If you're honest, he'll be fine."

"I hope you're right," Heather said.

The sound of a golf cart approaching caught her attention. Of course, Jim would park by the office and have someone drive him out here so he'd have to be escorted back to his vehicle. If she hadn't seen Jim's intentions before, she saw them now, and it was time to have a heart-to-heart with the resident vet because even if she didn't get to go on a date with Crew tonight.

She'd do it another night.

Her insides warmed as if she swallowed the sun.

She hadn't expected to feel such excitement over her pending evening festivities. It had been a good year since she'd gone out with anyone and her last relationship hadn't been anything to write home about. She'd gone through life in a haze of contentment that no longer served any purpose.

After she broke up with Shay, her entire adult life had been dedicated to her career. To the horses.

"Ah. Looks like my darling husband brought Jim." Cheyenne stood, keeping one hand on her growing belly.

Heather stepped into the middle of the barn. Izzy still lay in her stall, as did Dixon. Neither horse had the energy to stand on their own feet. Heather bent over and scratched behind Izzy's ears. "It's going to be okay, girl. The doc's here and he's going to find out what's troubling you."

"Hey, babe," Cheyenne said, greeting her husband, JB Whiskey. "Where's Jimmy?"

"He's at JW and Kitty's. We're all having dinner there tonight." JB wrapped his arm around his wife.

"Sounds great," Cheyenne said.

Heather kept her focus on Izzy and not the

doctor gathering his tools from the back of the golf cart.

This conversation was going to be harder than she thought. Hopefully, Cheyenne and JB would leave before Crew showed up; otherwise, the discussion wouldn't happen.

"Has there been any change in either of the horses?" Jim asked.

"Not really," Heather said. "They don't want to eat or drink and neither one has been able to get up all day."

"And there's been no dietary changes?" Jim took a long needle and prepared to inject the animal.

She cringed. While she knew this was necessary, it was as if he were about to poke her baby.

Izzy lowered her head into Heather's lap.

"There, there, girl. It's going to be okay." She continued to rub Izzy's nose.

"I'm going to give them a shot of antibiotics, but I want to get blood, urine, and stool samples. I also want to take a look at what they've been eating."

"We've already packed up some feed and a bushel of hay," Heather said. Nothing pained her more than when one of her animals was hurting and she couldn't make it better.

In her career, she'd lost a few horses to illness, and she'd even had to put a couple down.

But it never got easier to deal with.

Cheyenne squeezed her shoulder. "We're going to head out. Don't stay too long. Go. Enjoy your night with Crew."

Heather nodded. Though part of her wanted to spend the night right here in this barn. She kept her focus on the sick animal and not on Jim as he went about the business of attending to Izzy and Dixon.

Jim was the best at his profession. It's why the Whiskey family generally used Jim's services exclusively. Of course, the ranch was extensive and they had to use other vets on occasion, but Jim and his entire staff were on the Whiskey Ranch payroll. Jim knew animals and he knew how to treat sick ones.

Over the years, Heather and Jim had formed a professional bond and maybe, just maybe, she'd sent the wrong vibe since his love life had fallen apart when Bethany had left him and he'd cried on her shoulder, of all people, since Bethany was in love with another woman.

And that woman had been Heather.

Something Heather had never seen coming.

"I assume you've kept these two away from the rest of the animals?" Jim tossed his gloves into his bag.

"We have," Heather said. "I honestly thought it

was just a cold at first, but I'm thinking it's more serious."

"The horse flu is pretty bad this season. I was over at the Jetson farm the other day giving fluids to a few of their horses. I bet it's the same thing. Nothing for you to worry about." Jim flipped over a bucket and plopped his ass down. "You looked tired."

One thing she could count on Jim for was brutal honesty and that was something she appreciated about him. "It's been a long day," she admitted.

"It always is when you're taking care of sick creatures." He patted Izzy's bottom. "I hope you don't plan on staying here all night. You need to take care of yourself too."

"No. But we do have farmhands checking around the clock and they will call me if there are any changes."

"Make sure you let me know as well. I can be here at the drop of a hat." He rubbed the back of his neck. "Regardless, I'm going to give them some fluids tomorrow. I'll come by before I head into the office."

"About what time?"

"Around six."

"I'll let Annette know. She's usually the one here that early," Heather said. "I won't be too much later."

"No worries. I'll make sure I sign in and go

through all the proper channels. For now, their vitals are good and the antibiotic I gave them should help." He stood and held out his hand. "JB left the golf cart for me. I can give you a ride to wherever you're parked. Or better yet, why don't you let me buy you some dinner. You look like you need a good meal."

"Thanks, but I have plans tonight."

"I see," Jim said.

She nodded. Out of the corner of her eye, she saw Crew's Jeep bouncing down the dirt access road. She really needed more time to have this conversation with Jim, but if she didn't do it now, it wouldn't be fair to either man.

"You've been a good friend to me," she said.

"Ah. The dreaded friend zone."

"That's not a bad place to be," she said. "I've known you for twenty years and in all that time, we've only ever been friends."

He laughed. "But I've had a thing for you on and off for years, if you hadn't noticed."

Oh boy. She hadn't and that said a lot about her. Hell, she hadn't even noticed Shay at first and if there had ever been a man she'd been head over heels for, it had been Shay. "I'm sorry, but I don't see you that way."

"Is this how you told Bethany you didn't return her feelings?" His tone had changed slightly, reminding her of the hurt and humiliation Bethany had caused.

"That one really blindsided me."

"You and me both," Jim admitted. "I wanted her so badly to make friends in this town I didn't think to be jealous of a woman."

"Well, you do know nothing happened."

Jim nodded.

She pointed through the center of the barn toward where Crew rolled his SUV to a stop by the gate. She smiled and waved. Perspiration beaded across her palms. She wiped them on the front of her jeans. Crew had her body reacting in ways it hadn't since she was a twenty-year-old girl and she was still sneaking out to see Shay.

"Oh. That's right. I guess I did know you had a date with him." Jim took his bag in one hand and stuffed his other into his pocket. He strolled beside her as if he didn't have a care in the world. "I'm only saying this because I care about you."

"Jim. If you're going to talk badly about Crew, that's not cool."

"I've heard things about him and they are slightly disturbing."

"You know how I feel about gossip."

Jim ran a hand across his head. "I'm afraid what I know about him is all true."

"He's a cop and I doubt he's a bad one."

"No. He's a good cop. That I'm sure of." Jim paused by the golf cart. He reached out and took her hand. "But he's got a dark past."

"We all have one of those."

"You and I go back many years. I want only what's best for you and what makes you happy."

"I know that, Jim, but—"

"Whenever a woman says that word, it's never good." He lifted her hand and kissed the back of it. "I've grown to care about you deeply and in ways that go beyond friendship, as you now know. I thought you were feeling the same way, but you're not and I'm going to have to accept that so we can remain friends."

"I'm sorry. I want to keep things the way they are."

"I do too." Jim nodded. "And I want to believe Crew is a good man, but be careful. Make sure he treats you right and I will always be there for you, day or night. Remember that." He tossed his bag in the back of the cart.

"I didn't mean to hurt your feelings."

He ran his hand up and down her arm. "You didn't. I'll see you tomorrow."

"Thanks, Jim. I appreciate it."

"It's what I do." He hopped behind the steering

wheel and waved to Crew as he drove up the hill and toward the main building at the far end of the ranch.

Crew stepped from the vehicle, setting his Stetson on the seat. "Should I be jealous?"

She smiled. "He was just giving an injection to some sick horses." She strolled toward Crew with her legs feeling like Jell-O. No man had had this effect on her since she'd been in the eighth grade. "Unfortunately, I don't have a change of clothes and it's probably too late for me to go home and change only to go all the way back into town."

"This won't be a problem." He smiled like a big kid. "Other than Boone's place, I'm not big on going out to eat, so I was thinking, if you're up for it, we'd go on a picnic."

She tilted her head. "Seriously?"

He nodded. "I've got fried chicken and all the fixins back at my place."

"That's not a picnic. That's dinner at your home and that might be too much for a first date."

"It's warm, so we can eat outside." He held his hands up. "I'll be a gentleman. I promise."

"My car's over there." She pointed toward the main building where Jim was headed in his golf cart. "I'll follow you."

"Perfect." He grabbed his Stetson. "Now, hop in so I can take you to your vehicle."

4

*C*rew tossed his napkin to his plate and shoved it aside. Reaching across the table, he lifted the bottle of red wine and topped off both glasses.

Duke groaned as he rolled to his side in his bed while Daisy stood and stretched before making her way across the patio and sitting watch out over the mountains and the night sky.

"I've never seen dogs so well-mannered before," Heather said.

"I will say they are unusual, but I'm glad they are so mellow; otherwise, they'd drive me bonkers."

Heather leaned back in her chair. "That was almost as good as my sister's fried chicken." She raised her wine. Her pink lips curled over the rim.

He tried not to stare, but he couldn't tear his gaze

away. "I've had your sister, Reina's food when I stayed at your family's bed and breakfast when I first came to town. She's an amazing cook."

Heather nodded. "If I ate her food every day, I'd be six hundred pounds." She waved to her empty plate. "I'm impressed by your cooking skills."

"I don't do it very often." A thick frog caught in his throat. He was moving into territory that could end up changing the overall light feel of the evening and that was something he didn't want, but he wasn't sure if he could stop the slippery slope they were heading down.

"Why not?"

He shrugged. "I don't have a passion for it, I guess."

"When you have a sister who is a chef and cooks breakfast for the family and then lunch and dinner for everyone on the ranch, you pretty much never have to cook."

"My late wife loved to cook and she used to make me do it with her. She used to tell me that if we could handle cooking together, we could handle anything." He shrugged. "The joy of cooking kind of rubbed off on me." Wow. The words just tumbled out of his mouth as if it were an everyday occurrence for him to discuss Darla, a topic never discussed with anyone. His emotions were too raw and the rage too close to the surface to allow her name to slip from his lips during casual conversation.

But everything was different with Heather. He found himself feeling as though he could handle late afternoon strolls through the center of town with his hand on the center of her back while everyone stared and whispered.

And he wouldn't care.

Well, actually, that wasn't true.

He would absolutely care because he'd want them looking. He'd want them thinking that he was the luckiest man in all of Idaho because Heather was by his side.

He'd lost his mind. Perhaps men did have needs and they didn't come in the shape of their right hand.

"Your wife passed?" Heather tilted her head. The sparkle in her light-blue eyes faltered as it did with most people when he brought up Darla. Whether they knew anything about Darla or not, they always gave what he referred to as the head tilt and bob, showing off the fact they had no idea what to say or do because there was no logical response to what he'd suffered except for *that's fucked up*.

However, no one ever said those words because everyone thought that would be screwed up.

"She did," he said, not knowing how else to respond. What else was there to say?

"I'm so sorry for your loss." She swirled the wine, letting it hug the sides of the glass. Her gaze followed the movement as if it were telling her a story. "Is that why you moved here?"

That was a loaded question and he wasn't sure how honest he should be, if at all. He'd never told anyone in these parts, except for his boss, what happened. And he hadn't talked about his family to anyone except for Darla's sister and her family and that never went over well.

The world blamed him and for the most part, he understood why.

Of course, Heather could google his name along with his hometown and she'd get a week's worth of reading material on *The Artist*, the serial killer that murdered his wife and daughter along with twenty-five other young women.

That would be a shitty way for her to find out about his past.

It surprised Crew that half the town didn't already know. He hadn't changed his name or his history. When he first came to town, he wanted people to know. He wanted everyone to point and stare. He thought that if they knew the ugly truth, they'd have to run him out of town.

But that didn't happen.

Either they didn't care, or they didn't know. He suspected it was a combination of the two, depending on who possessed the knowledge. And of course, there was always the idea that some knew but didn't feel like bringing it to Crew's attention.

Smart on their part.

"That's one of the many reasons and I'm surprised you didn't already know that I'd been married."

"I'm sorry. I shouldn't have asked such a personal question." She took a long strand of her hair and twisted it between her fingers. The dark locks sparkled under the glare of the white moon shining bright in the dark Idaho sky.

"It's fine. I'm kind of surprised more people don't ask about my past."

She let out a short laugh. "Besides you being a cop and that makes people a little afraid. You give off a kind of scary, introverted-type vibe, which makes everyone keep their distance."

He arched a playful brow. "You don't say."

The corner of her mouth tipped upward. "You like it when folks are intimidated."

"It does help me do my job," he admitted. "I prefer the word respect, but not everyone respects the uniform."

"And I've never seen you wear one." She waggled her finger. "So, it makes it hard to honor that."

"Yeah. I'm not a fan of the blue and so far my boss at the police department doesn't push me to wear it when I'm on patrol, though I bet if someone complained, I'd be screwed."

"It pisses Steven off."

"Everything bugs that man, but not enough to bitch to the higher-ups. At least he does it to my face. I give him kudos for that." In the last two years, Crew couldn't remember when he'd had such an enjoyable evening. There'd been twitches of happiness. Moments where he'd felt a pang of what it was like to be alive, but since he'd lost his family, he'd never had even a minute where he thought life could be something worth tuning in for.

Until right this second.

Something about Heather made him want to check in and see if the world had anything worth opening his eyes for.

And Heather was certainly a good start.

"And the fact that he hasn't gone around blasting my personal business to the town, since he knows my wife died."

"Oh, he's gossiped about you; he's just never said anything about that."

Crew arched a brow. "And what has he said, exactly?"

"I only know what my sister says, which isn't much, but there is some chatter about why you left a big city to come be a detective in a small town."

"Of course he would. I swear he has a perpetual stick up his ass," Crew said. "But he's a good cop and not bad to work with."

"I can't say he says the same about you." Heather's pink tongue darted out from between her lips and made a broad stroke across her mouth. "I'm sorry. I shouldn't have told you that. Steven gets jealous easily."

"I can see that." Crew resented how she affected him on such a primal level, but only because he couldn't just have sex with her and walk away. His conscience wouldn't allow it. She was too kind. Too sweet. And too intellectually stimulating. She was the kind of woman that deserved better than a one-night stand and he didn't get involved with women that he couldn't walk away from.

Emotional ties were not anything he could tolerate.

"I'm sure he thinks I'm an asshole and out for his job." Crew had butted heads with Steven and everyone else in the police department. No one liked the way Crew did things and that's because Crew still didn't like to follow the rule book.

Rules were meant to be adjusted to work for the system as needed.

A concept that nearly got him fired more than once and one that had him on thin ice with his current employer. So far, he'd been doing everything by the book, except the uniform thing.

That he couldn't get on board with.

"Why do you say that?" Heather asked.

"Because he's called me that a time or two." Crew stacked the dishes on top of each other. "I'm used to keeping people at a distance and by doing that I tend to come off as abrupt and rude."

"Here. Let me do that. It's the least I can do." She curled her fingers around the edges of the plates. Her skin touching his, igniting it, sending shock-waves across his body.

A warmth spread from his hands to his gut. He felt like he was twelve years old again and about to kiss a girl for the first time. "No. You're my guest. I'm just going to set them in the sink and get the pie."

"You will do no such thing. If this stuff sits much longer it will take forever to get off. We'll do it now and then have pie. Deal?"

"Yes, ma'am," he said.

"And if you call me that ever again," Heather said.

"I'll do as my grandmama used to do and smack you upside the head." She gave him a gentle tap. "Get the picture?"

"Loud and clear." He glanced at his dogs. "You two, sit and stay."

They both groaned.

"Wow. They are really well trained."

"They have their moments." He hadn't had this much fun since...well...since before his wife had passed. Darla had always managed to make him smile, even when he'd been in the worst of moods.

He followed Heather into his kitchen and set the dirty dishes next to the sink. He started on the washing while she did the drying. It took all of ten minutes to clean up and when they were done, he pulled his homemade apple pie from the oven that he'd been heating up. "Ice cream?"

"Do you really have to ask?" She turned and ran her fingers over the counter as she glanced out into his family room.

His heartbeat raced. He'd never had anyone inside his rented home, which sat about two miles outside of town. Close enough that it only took him ten minutes to get to work, but far enough away that the townsfolk weren't passing by while he was front porch sitting, or would be gossiping about his visitor.

55

Well, at least he hoped that would be the case.

However, what concerned him right this moment were the pictures displayed on the hallway wall.

He set the pie on the counter and took down two plates, quickly cutting into and giving them each a good-sized portion. "Shall we go back outside?" He hadn't thought this through when he'd decided on a picnic.

"Okay," she said softly.

He picked up the plates and headed toward the sliding glass doors. He glanced over his shoulder and paused.

Heather stood in the middle of the hallway with her fingertips on one of the pictures of Darla and Gypsy.

Setting the decadent dessert on the table, he made his way through the house and stood behind Heather. He reached out and lifted the image off the wall. "This was taken about six months before they were killed."

"They?"

"My wife Darla and my daughter Gypsy. They were murdered." His heart turned to stone. It was as if the blood in his veins dried up. His lungs burned with rage. It didn't matter that their killer had been brought to justice. It gave Crew no peace of mind that no one else would suffer at the hands of *The*

Artist. All it did was remind Crew that he brought that killer to his doorstep and he caused his own family's demise. He placed the picture back on the wall and took a step back. He'd filled his home with reminders of his past life because he needed to be reminded.

The second his eyes opened, the pain jabbed at his body like those fish used at a foot spa to clean off the dead skin. The pictures intensified that anguish like pouring rubbing alcohol on an open wound.

He lived for that sensation.

"Did they catch whoever killed them?" Heather asked with wide eyes.

He nodded. "I did, but that doesn't change the fact they were brutally murdered." And it was all his fault. Hell, he might as well have stuck the knife in their bodies.

Heather reached up and palmed his cheek. "Does it help?"

"Not really." He took her wrist. "And I'd rather not talk about it." He took in a slow breath, doing his best to thaw out his frozen heart. There was no reason for him to treat Heather with anything other than kindness. She didn't know his history and she didn't deserve his wrath. "I'm sorry."

"Oh, Crew. I'm the one who should be apologizing." She held his hands between hers and squeezed.

"That pie smells delicious." She sidestepped him and snagged one of the plates.

He glanced over his shoulder. Gypsy had been the apple of his eye. The sweetest little girl in the world. Every time he'd come home from work, she'd race to the door with her arms wide open. In her eyes, Crew could do no wrong.

"I'm trying, baby girl, I really am," he whispered. He made his way back outside and joined Heather under the stars. Spring in Idaho wasn't much different than Michigan, only the night sky seemed vaster. Wider. Brighter. "Thank you." He placed his plate on the table and dug in.

"For what?"

"For letting me have my crazy rude moment." He waved his spoon in the air. "No one really knows about my family and I'm never in a good mood when I discuss them."

"It's understandable," she said. "I didn't mean to pry."

"You didn't. I have pictures of Darla and Gypsy on display everywhere. To be totally honest, I've never had anyone over since I moved here, and I didn't think I'd ever have anyone inside."

Heather nodded. "You don't have to explain yourself to me."

He blew out a puff of air. "I feel like I do." He lifted the bottle of wine.

"No more for me. I have to drive home."

"Hope you don't mind if I finish it off." He needed a shot of courage because for some strange reason, he wanted to be honest with Heather.

"Not at all."

"I haven't really dated since they were killed and that was a little over two years ago." He stared at the sky, as if the stars and the moon would guide him as to what to say. "I was in a really dark place for a while and most people didn't think I'd make it back. Hell, at one point, I wanted to die myself." He really shouldn't be telling Heather any of this. It wasn't first date material.

It wasn't date material, period.

"I can't imagine how horrible that must have been for you, or how hard it's been to try to recover from. I suspect it's a struggle every day."

That was not the response he suspected. Most people told him how it would get better and that they understood his anguish when in reality, they didn't know jack shit.

"It's not easy, that's for sure." He rubbed his temple. The few times he did get into this conversation with anyone, he did his best not to be a total dickhead. He was used to using his tortured soul to push people away. In general, no one knew how to deal with that kind of grief, and Crew had learned to use it as a form of protection from the world.

As a way to keep everyone out and a piece of the darkness close to his heart.

Only, Heather made him want to change that and he wasn't sure what to do with that new sensation.

Or how to deal with Heather and the emotional upheaval she created.

"I came here because I thought I could fade into the background. I thought I could be seen, but not really."

"That never happens in a small town. Not even for those who live out in the middle of nowhere and almost never come into the village. We all still know what happens in their lives."

"I'm learning that the hard way," he said with amusement stirring in his gut. "You're a breath of fresh air and totally unexpected."

"I think that's a compliment."

"It is."

"And this pie is the best thing I've ever had in my mouth."

"I hope that's not true." He blinked slowly. "I can't believe I just said that."

"You're a man. I'm not shocked."

He licked the spoon. "I'm sorry I ruined our date."

"You didn't ruin anything." Heather reached out across the table and squeezed his hand. "I've had a really good time. Actually, I haven't had this much fun in forever."

"So good you want to repeat it?" Shit. That was a horrible way to ask for a second date.

"I'm not a huge fan of public dating," she said.

He coughed. "I'm not sure what that means."

"Whenever I go out with a guy the first few times, it's always at a restaurant or at a party and I always feel like I'm on display for the world to judge and it's gross. It puts me on the defensive and the dates never end well."

"I have the opposite problem. The times I've gone out, I prefer them to be in public. That way my family won't enter the conversation, or I can't turn into a jerk, saying something stupid, putting a damper on the evening." He lowered his chin and raised his finger. "Then again, this is honestly only my third date since my wife passed away."

"I'm dying to know who else you've taken out," Heather said with a playful smirk.

"No one from around here." Crew's emotions ran hot and cold. On the one hand, he enjoyed Heather's company. It was as if they were old friends and he didn't struggle to maintain calm, even when his worst memories were taunting him. "What about you? You're a beautiful and intelligent woman. I'm shocked you don't have a boyfriend." He found himself wanting to know about her past, and that was dangerous territory. "I'm sure the men of this town are dropping at your feet."

She cocked her head. "I wouldn't go that far."

"Come on. You couldn't have gone your whole life so far and not have had at least one long-term relationship."

She leaned forward, resting her elbows on the table. "Have you met Shay Killian?"

"The EMT?" Crew asked. "I have. A few times."

"We were engaged for five minutes."

Crew arched a brow. That was a union he hadn't expected. "How long ago?"

"About ten years."

"You must have been really young. What happened?" Crew shifted in his seat, waiting for the uncomfortable feeling to overtake his mind and body. He shouldn't feel this at ease with Heather.

And he should be calling it a night, instead of letting one sexy lady break through his carefully constructed wall of protection.

"We were about twenty-three when we broke up." She shook her head. "Too young to know what we were doing, but I was pregnant and we thought that was the right next step."

"Oh." His heart dropped to the pit of his stomach. He understood how a child could change everything. Having Gypsy certainly turned his world upside down, but for the better. When his little girl's hopes and dreams were stolen by *The Artist*, Crew wasn't sure he'd ever want to see his surroundings in color again. Nothing mattered but his Gypsy and his sweet Darla and now they were gone, leaving him a shell of a man with little purpose. Work filled a tiny portion of that void and he thought he could go through the rest of his existence half a person.

However, Heather made those empty spaces crave human contact.

The very thing he'd moved to this small town to avoid.

She placed her hand over her middle. "I lost the baby in the fourth month. It was a fluke thing. There was nothing anyone could have done. Only, it was Jim who saved my life."

"Seriously?"

She nodded. "The placenta had abrupted and I started—shit—you don't want hear this."

"Actually, I do."

She blew out a slow breath. "I was on the ranch and was bleeding. Hemorrhaging. Jim happened to be there attending to a sick cow. He couldn't save the baby. Or my ability to have children, but he did save me."

"I'm so sorry." A sharp pain tore through his heart. Losing a child, even a promise of a child could destroy a person.

"Thank you." She nodded. "Anyway. While Shay and I loved each other, we weren't ready to get married much less have a kid together. And losing our baby was hard enough. Knowing we'd never have children was too much for us. I used it as a reason to go our separate ways since it was the baby that forced our hand and he's never really forgiven me for not fighting for us, but I think part of him blames me."

"Death has a way of doing that to people." The corners of his eyes burned. Bonding with other humans always took its toll on Crew. He didn't like doing it often and connecting to Heather this way made him want her even more.

"Shay and I have been able to remain friends, but it took a while to get there and it's a bit strained at times. I know he wants to have a family in the worst way, so I struggle with why he keeps Fiona at arm's length. The two of them are perfect for each other, but they don't get it."

"A lot of couples don't make it through a loss like that, but look at you playing matchmaker."

"I just want him to be happy."

"And are you?" Who was Crew to question anyone's level of happiness when he couldn't even say he was content. "What have you been doing for yourself since then?"

"I've focused all my attention on my career and standing on my own two feet." She tossed her hair over her shoulder. "When I found out I was pregnant, I wasn't sure I wanted to keep it."

"That's fair. It's your body."

"Shay's family doesn't quite think that way. Nor does mine, for that matter, but once I gave myself a chance to accept the reality, I fell in love with the idea. When I miscarried, I was devastated, but not enough to continue with the engagement and to try again. I realized that I just wasn't ready and until a couple of years ago, I had no desire to be in a committed relationship."

"So, that begs the question, who has been in your life the last year or so?"

"A bunch of horses, a couple of cows, and a pig named Tully."

"And a vet named Jim who really does care about you."

"Him too," she said with a long breath. "We're just friends and he feels protective of me considering what he saw me go through."

"I'm not sure he sees it that way, and I'm not the kind of guy who chases a girl." Crew hadn't meant to sound so harsh, but he didn't want to get into a pissing match with Jim over Heather. If there was any chance that Heather would prefer Jim over him, then this would be the moment for her to walk away.

She tilted her head. "I'm not asking for anyone to *chase* me."

He reached down and scratched his dog's head. "Not quite how I meant to put that."

"What exactly did you mean, then?"

"I'm not sure I know how to say this without being rude." Duke shifted, grunting as if to tell Crew to stop talking because he was fucking up so badly.

But that had been Crew's intent. Put the brakes on. Make a U-turn. Get her to tell him to hit the road. Anything to prevent him from peeling back another layer of his own onion. Being more vulnerable was the last thing he needed.

However, being an asshole wasn't what she needed.

"It's one thing if you want him to go away and you're using me to achieve that goal, but if that's the case—"

"That's not what I'm doing and I'm sorry if it came across that way." She held up a hand. "Jim was there for me when I lost my baby. He was a good friend and stood by me when I left Shay where others judged me pretty harshly and I've been there for him when it comes to Bethany."

"His ex-fiancée?" Crew had asked around a little bit about her and no one seems to know what happened or why she left town.

Heather nodded.

"What happened with those two?" he asked.

"It's not my story to tell," she said.

"You just told me about Shay."

She cocked her head. "But that directly affected me. This doesn't. Not really. And I promised him I wouldn't ever tell anyone. I'm sorry. I couldn't do that to Jim. Just like he wouldn't tell you, or any other man I might date, that I can't have children."

He opened his mouth, but snapped it shut. She had a valid point. She'd shared something incredibly painful about her past, present, and future. He had no right to ask her to break a confidence. "You're a good friend, considering that the rumor mills around this town link his breakup to you." He held his hand up. "However, knowing your part of the history, which I'm to assume most of this town doesn't know the end result of the miscarriage, I understand why you defend him so readily."

"The only people who know are Jim, my immediate family, and Shay. Not even his folks or Zuri know I no longer have a uterus. It's no one else's business and I have no idea why I just told you." She dabbed her eyes. "I'm sorry. It's getting late and I really should head home."

"On our next date remind me not to bring up Jim."

"So, you want to go out again?"

"I do."

"Sounds like fun to me." She laughed.

He stood, stretching out his arm.

She took the hand he offered and followed him through the house to the front door.

"So, how about on Sunday afternoon we go to the Whiskey Ranch showcase together," he said.

"That's a pretty public date."

"I know but maybe we both need to start changing the way everyone sees us individually." He leaned in and kissed her cheek. "And together."

She smiled. "Consider it a date."

He ran his hands up and down her biceps, staring into her seductive chocolate orbs. "All I want to do is kiss you right now."

Her lashes fluttered seductively over her warm orbs. Everything about her drew him in like the beams of a lighthouse showing the way home.

She raised up on tiptoe and pressed her mouth

over his. Her tongue darted between his lips, sending a warm shiver through his body, waking up the parts of him that he thought were dead.

He heaved her to his chest, wrapping his arm around her tiny waist, and he shoved her against the porch railing, ramming his knee between her legs. His mind screamed at him to slow down. That she was a lady and he needed to treat her accordingly.

However, when she locked her ankles around his backside, all bets were off.

Until something vibrated against his side.

He jumped. "What the hell was that?" He set her feet down on the floor.

She held up her clutch purse with a slight laugh. "My phone." Her smile turned into a frown.

"What's wrong?"

"Just an update on the sick horses." She let out a long breath. "They are doing better, but I should probably go. I want to stop by the ranch and check on them."

He nodded. "That was about to get out of hand."

"But it didn't."

"But I wanted it to, and I'm not sure I would have stopped it had your phone not freaked me out."

"I have no idea if I would have either, but we both just put the brakes on." She smiled. "About Sunday. I have to be at the ranch really early, so you'll have to meet me there. Just text me when you're through the gate. I'll make sure you have a backstage pass."

"What if I want to see you before Sunday?" He tucked a piece of her hair behind her ear.

"You've got my number." With that, she turned on her heel and strolled down the path. She paused by her vehicle and waved.

Crew patted his chest and smiled.

Daisy pushed her nose against his hand. He glanced down. "What the hell am I going to do, girl?" He scratched Daisy's ears. "I think Heather has the ability to put my heart back together again, only to crush it."

5

"*L*ook at you standing up on your own four feet." Heather held out a slice of apple, thankful that Izzy took it in her mouth and chewed.

"Both seem to be doing much better," Jim said, patting the horse on the backside. "But I need to talk to you about what I found." He glanced over his shoulder before waving his hand out in front. "Why don't we step outside."

She narrowed her stare. The only other people in the barn were Cheyenne and Fiona, another trainer at Whiskey Ranch. He could speak freely in front of them.

Hell, he should be keeping Cheyenne in the loop. Her husband was one of the owners and they all reported to Annette, who was also married to an owner.

"Okay, but don't you think we should have Cheyenne come with us?"

Jim curled his fingers, digging a little too firmly around her forearm, and guided her through the open barn and into the clearing.

The sun peeked out through a big white puffy cloud. The warm rays landed on her face, spreading heat across her skin like she'd just stepped under a waterfall.

"When I got here this morning, both Izzy's and Dixon's stalls were open. They were wandering in with the other horses in the main corral."

"What time was that?" She glanced at her watch. She'd arrived at the ranch around six thirty in the morning and the staff had already signed Jim onto the premises. No one mentioned anything about any of the stalls being open or any of the sick horses having mingled with the healthy ones.

Besides, she'd stopped by herself and everything was locked up nice and tight at midnight.

And if it had been after that, she would have been notified by someone and not the vet.

"I arrived just a little after six and while I was thrilled to see Izzy and Dixon on their feet, having them share water from the same barrel with healthy horses could cause a mass infection of every animal in this barn."

"I'm well aware," Heather said, annoyed by Jim's tone. "I'll have to talk to the staff."

"The night staff didn't want to get you in trouble with your boss. They said you stopped by last night, but when I looked, it's not on the books."

"I don't have to sign in as a trainer." Heather arched a brow. Heat crawled from her gut to her cheeks, and not from embarrassment. No way had she forgotten to close the stalls.

And what the hell was Jim implying? That she'd done it on purpose?

"I'm just repeating what I'm being told and that some are concerned that your head isn't in the right space."

"That's impossible."

"I'm certainly not going to say anything and I'm sure it's all bullshit, but I wanted you to know." Jim held up his hand. "I took some more cultures and so far everything is coming back that they both had some sort of stomach bug and should be fine in a day or two. I'd still keep them isolated from the rest of the animals. I'll be back at the end of the day."

"I appreciate it, but I can't leave things like this, Jim. I need to know who said the gates were open."

Jim rubbed the back of his neck. "Everyone

except your bosses, but you didn't hear that from me and it's not the only thing they are saying."

"Excuse me?"

"They gave me some feed. Moldy feed that they said you fed Izzy yesterday right before you left with Crew. They said you knew it because it was the feed you had set aside to be tossed, but you couldn't be bothered to go down—"

She waved her hand. "I've heard enough and that's all fucking lies and you know it. I'd never knowingly hurt an animal."

"I suspect you were just distracted by your date."

She narrowed her eyes. "I was not. How dare you. Come on. You know me better than that. Where the hell is this coming from?"

Jim took out a handkerchief and wiped his brow. "Look. I have to get going, but I'd like to talk to you more about this. Do you have any plans tonight?" He tossed his bag on the back of the golf cart.

"Nothing specific."

"That new guy is going to be singing over at Boone's tonight. Why don't we go over there, that way no one here will be concerned about us talking with each other and I can tell you everything that was expressed to me." He leaned against the hood. "I know you're dating Crew. I'm not asking you on date, just so you know."

74

"For the record, I'm not dating Crew." Not that it was any of Jim's business who she dated, but she felt the need to clarify.

"But you're interested," Jim said. "And I respect that. However, I think you need to know some things about how people see you now that they think you're seeing the moody resident detective with a dark history." He slipped behind the steering wheel. "So how about it? You have to eat."

"I don't know. I've got a long day ahead of me."

"Just think about it. You can let me know when I get back." He turned the key and punched the gas. He waved as the tires kicked up dirt.

She hugged her middle and took a step back.

Did he really just concoct some lie to get her to go out with him? That was weird. And desperate.

Or were people talking about her behind her back? And what the hell was going on with the open gates and moldy feed?

"What the hell was that all about?"

Heather jumped at the sound of Fiona's voice. "Jesus. You scared the crap out of me."

"Sorry," Fiona said. "What did he want with you out here all alone?"

"He wanted to talk to me about the gates being open this morning and to ask me to drinks tonight at Boone's place," Heather admitted.

"What gates?"

"Jim said Izzy and Dixon were in the main corral when he got here." Heather wasn't sure how much she should tell Fiona. Not that Fiona would gossip with Jim, but the whole thing was just weird, and Heather wanted some time to make sense of it.

"I got here before you and I didn't notice that, but Jim was here before me and the night stall boy, Carl, was acting all weird." Fiona shrugged.

"Weird, how?"

"Like he got caught with his hand in the cookie jar. I figured he went riding or something. He's done that before. Or maybe had a girl up and had sex somewhere."

"Gross," Heather said. "People still do that?"

Fiona laughed. "Come on. What young ranch hand hasn't used working for the Whiskey brothers to get laid?"

"Hey, some of you girl ranch hands have used it too." Heather pursed her lips. "Someone should have a chat with Carl and it shouldn't be me. Not if he's trying to place blame for something he did, knowing I came back last night."

"I'm not staying late, but I will check with Annette."

"Thanks, she'll know how to handle that one. Now,

how about going with me to Boone's tonight?" She had it under good authority that Crew would be there, and she really wanted to see him—no—kiss him again.

It was time for her to move beyond the agony of what she'd lost and hanging out with Crew was a step in that direction. The irony there had been she hadn't planned on getting married or having a family. She hadn't ever thought about having kids.

At least not in her early twenties. No. All she could really think about back then had been making a name for herself at Whiskey Ranch. She was an up-and-coming trainer and she needed to carve out a space for herself, not get pushed aside because she had a husband and a kid to take care of and that attitude had been what destroyed her relationship with Shay.

Not the miscarriage.

Though, not ever being able to have children certainly changed things.

And now, even if she wanted to have a family of her own, she couldn't.

Fiona waggled her brows. "Well, now. Are we burning both ends of the candle? Because I could have sworn I heard Jim say he was going to be there and I know Crew is going to be there, so what is this game you're playing?"

"Jim says people are talking about me and I want to know what they are saying."

Fiona tilted her head. "Are you sure that's not just a ploy to get you at a bar with a drink in your hand where Crew might see you?"

"Jim's not that childish."

"Yes, he is," Fiona laughed. "But you know what, I wouldn't say no to going on a date with Jim," Fiona said.

"You would just be using him to make Shay jealous."

"I could kiss another man right in front of Shay and he wouldn't care." Fiona hopped up on the fence, taking her Stetson and resting it on her lap. "Jim wouldn't be the worst catch in this town."

"You're in love with Shay."

Fiona laughed. "I can't decide if he's still hung up on you or if he's gay."

"He's definitely not gay and he's not in love with me either."

"Maybe not, but you did a number on him." Fiona's words had a trace of disdain covered in a dollop of sugar.

"The loss of our baby, among other things, did that." Though Heather wasn't entirely sure what Shay's hang-ups were because he'd said many times he wasn't in love with her and he wished her well.

And she believed him.

"Why are you bringing this up? You're acting like I did something to you personally."

"You kind of did," Fiona said. "I mean, three of the sexiest single men in this town all have it bad for you and you're dicking them all around." Fiona held up her hand. "I mean that in the best girlfriend way."

"I take offense to that no matter what spin you try to put on it." If Heather had to pick a best friend, she'd pick Fiona. They went all the way back to kindergarten and Fiona knew everything about Heather.

Well, not everything.

"Not a spin," Fiona said. "Just stating the facts. Shay's still hung up on what happened. He says he's not, but the last time we went out, all he did was stare at the family sitting next to us. I figured I'd take his mind off it by climbing under the table."

"Oh, my God. You didn't."

Fiona rolled her eyes. "You know I did, and you know he loved every second of it. It worked too, until I told him that maybe he should think about settling down. Perhaps with a nice girl like me, and that's when he burst out laughing, and I got all mad and walked away. That was a few weeks ago."

"You haven't spoken since?"

"Nope. And he hasn't even tried to reach out

and honestly, I'm over it. I thought maybe I'd go and ask out the new dark and dreamy detective, but this whole town is gossiping about how you were at his house last night and between the big kiss in front of Boone's, and sucking face on Crew's porch—"

"Excuse me?" Heather took her braid and twisted it between her fingers. She glanced over her shoulder toward the main administration building. Jim had parked the golf cart back in its spot and was currently standing in the parking lot speaking with JD Whiskey.

She couldn't help but wonder what that conversation was all about, but currently she wanted to know who was saying what about her and Crew.

"Are you going to deny you spent the night with Crew?"

"I absolutely am." She folded her arms. "I had dinner at his house, but I left around nine."

"I heard you snuck out at five this morning." Fiona waggled her brows. "I'm a little annoyed you didn't tell me."

"There is nothing to tell because I didn't sleep with Crew." Heather pinched the bridge of her nose. "Now, please, who is spreading that rumor?"

"Ashley said she saw you in a passionate embrace." Fiona crinkled her brow.

"I did kiss him, but it was when I left, the night before."

Ashley Allen was the resident weather person on the local morning show. She also used to be Bethany's best friend who had been engaged to Jim.

"When did you see Ashley for her to tell you this?" Considering it was still early, it didn't make sense that the gossip mills would have already started.

"I ran into her when I stopped at Maxie's to get a couple dozen doughnuts and some boxes of coffee. She was there picking up stuff for an office meeting and she asked what I knew and of course, I tried to pretend I wasn't too shocked, since you are my best friend."

"Fuck. So, you let her think I snuck out of our resident detective's home and did the walk of shame this morning?"

"Why would she lie about what she saw?"

"I don't know, but it wasn't me." Perhaps someone else with a similar car left Crew's house this morning. Which meant maybe he was seeing someone else.

He had every right to date whomever he wanted. He owed her nothing.

Either way, the entire thing could be cleared up with a conversation, though that wouldn't stop the

81

gossips. Nothing could prevent people from talking behind her back, something she'd gotten used to over the years.

"Well, shit. I'm sorry," Fiona said. "I didn't know. I mean. The man's hot. You're single and you do need to get laid, and damn, what a shitty thing for him to do."

"What do you mean?"

"If you're dating him and he goes off and screws—"

Heather held up her index finger. "First, I'm not dating him. Second, he can take to bed anyone he wants."

"Including me?"

"No. You're off-limits," Heather said slightly tongue in cheek.

"Oh. So you do like him."

Heather's pulse increased. "Just a little bit, so I'd rather not compete with the likes of you."

"So, that leaves Jim." Fiona sighed.

"Seriously? You're going to settle when we both know it's Shay you really want." Heather had been doing this dance with Fiona for the last year and Heather really wished she understood why Shay kept pushing Fiona away. They were perfect for one another, but Heather wouldn't get involved. Not when it involved Shay.

That would only cause more problems and she wouldn't do that to Fiona.

"I'm not settling." Fiona took her Stetson and pressed it on her head. "I'm tired of waiting for Shay to get his shit together. If he can't understand that he needs to make more of an effort and that I want more, then I'm done with him and ready to move on. Jim is a good man with an excellent career. The only negative is he's got a thing for you." She shook her head. "Story of my fucking life when it comes to men."

"I think you're going after the wrong man." Heather stretched out her arm and took her friend's hand. "You should reach out to Shay and have a conversation with him."

"My ego couldn't handle the rejection." Fiona slid from the fence. "Shall I ask Ashley about what she really saw?"

"No. I'll handle that." And Heather would. But she'd do it on her terms because at the end of the day, if Crew wanted to have his cake and eat it too, he was going to have to find a different flavor.

6

One of the things Crew missed about living in a big city was the variety of pubs and bars where he could grab a bite and blend into the background.

He couldn't do that at Boone's. However, he did enjoy knowing he'd always have a table, or at the very least a seat at the bar when he entered this fine establishment. Boone was good to the locals that way and if there was a long wait, someone always gave up their seat for him, or any other first responder that entered. Not a single person ever did that in Detroit.

Ever.

He stepped into the main room and inhaled sharply. All the rich flavors from frying potatoes to grilling meats assaulted his senses. His stomach growled as he scanned the restaurant, his gaze landing on the beautiful woman who visited his dreams.

Crew hadn't anticipated seeing Heather at Boone's, much less having pangs of jealously seeing her at a table with Jim along with her friend Zuri and a young woman he'd seen around town and up at Whiskey Ranch, though for the life of him, he couldn't remember her name.

It started with an *F*, but that's all he knew.

He was about to nonchalantly wander across the bar and interrupt the conversation, but Boone and his lovely wife stepped in his path.

"Hey, Boone. Hey, Paget. How are you both this fine night?" Crew put on his best smile. The one where no one could accuse him of being aloof.

A word he'd never used before moving to Buhl and one that had been used to describe him at least a dozen times.

"Doing great," Boone said. "I'm always happy when my beautiful wife is on my arm."

Paget patted her belly and laughed. "Boone's car is in the shop, so he needed me to come pick him up."

Boone shrugged. "I'm still happier when you're here than when you're not and everyone will attest to that." He leaned in and kissed her cheek.

"Flattery will get you anything you want, dear."

Boone laughed. "Crew, would you like a table at the bar or out on the back patio?"

Crew glanced around the room. He shouldn't do it. Being close to Heather wouldn't do him any good. She was with her friends and Jim.

Gross Jim.

Shit.

The man wasn't gross. He was just proving to be a pain in the ass.

"Is it okay if I take that empty table right there?" Crew asked.

"Not a problem." Boone waved to one of the waitresses. "Sawyer won't be starting for an hour, if you were looking to listen to some of his awesome music."

"I'll be eating and scooting out the door, so I won't be very long." He pointed to the badge hanging on his shirt. "I'm on duty and just needed to refuel."

"I completely understand." Boone squeezed his shoulder. "Would you mind keeping my wife company for fifteen minutes or so? I've got to deal with some business things."

"I can't think of a prettier person to spend some time with." Crew tipped his head. "I'd love to keep Paget company."

"Oh good," Paget said. "Not that I can't handle

myself in this place, but it will be nice to sit and have a quiet conversation with someone who doesn't work on the ranch or work for my husband."

Crew followed Boone and his wife to a small table about three away from Heather, her friend—Fiona—that was her name, Zuri, and Jim.

Shit. Crew was getting quite testy over the nice vet when he shouldn't be. The man had saved Heather's life. They had a unique friendship. There was no reason for Crew to have any animosity over the situation whatsoever.

So this feeling sitting in the pit of his stomach like a cylinder block tossed over a boat plummeting to the bottom of the ocean meant nothing.

Nada.

Zilch.

Boone kissed Paget before pulling out a chair. "I won't be too long. I promise."

"I'm in good company." Paget smiled, leaning forward, resting her face in her hands. "So, tell me why my co-worker keeps glancing in this direction with a questioning gaze."

"What does a questioning gaze look like?" He did his best not to turn his attention toward Heather, but that proved to be impossible. He lowered his chin and waved, noting if looks could kill, he'd be mortally wounded. "Never mind. I get it now and I have no idea."

"I've never really understood her and Jim. I mean, they don't act like they are close friends, but they have an odd relationship."

"Have they ever dated?" Fuck. Why did he have to go and ask such a stupid question. It implied he had an interest, and while he did, he wasn't going to act on it. He couldn't. He'd made that decision this morning when Ashley had randomly stopped by wondering if he wanted to go for coffee and doughnuts.

Who did that at five in the morning and just because he was standing on his front porch didn't mean he wanted visitors. Using the excuse she wanted to ask him about harassing text messages from a man she'd met online was lame at best. Especially when, from what he could tell, she was enjoying not only the attention, but she was encouraging this man to continue the conversation.

What was even weirder was when Ashley brought up both Jim and Heather. Not only had the segue not made much sense, but he thought it odd that she'd want to discuss either of them.

"Not to my knowledge."

"You mean it's possible?"

"Anything is possible with Heather," Paget said.

"I mean, Jim's not her type. But they are friends. And Heather is a private woman, especially after what happened with Shay, so I wouldn't be surprised if she's dated people without anyone knowing."

"Do you think she's not over Shay?"

"No. She and Shay were done before they even began, though there are probably still a lot of hurt feelings on both parts." Paget took a piece of bread that the waitress had set on the table and broke it in half, plopping some of it in her mouth. "Truthfully, Heather has some heartbreak in her life that some people just don't easily get over."

"I can relate to that."

"You certainly have a lot of questions regarding my co-worker." Paget lifted the glass of water and swigged. "And the resident vet. I'm starting to think you're jealous right now."

"I wouldn't go that far." Crew had become distrustful of Jim and his intentions toward Heather, and that was a concept Crew wanted to shake. Even if Heather was his girlfriend, this kind of emotion was useless and only caused emotional distraught. He needed to push past it, regardless.

Paget smiled. "Do you have eyes for Heather? Because from where I'm sitting, I'd say you're interested."

"I'm curious." Crew lowered his chin. "As in my profession makes me wonder about her."

"Are you *wondering* about anyone else?" Paget winked.

Crew laughed. "Not at the moment." He hadn't made too many friends since he moved to town, but he'd consider Boone and his bride a little more than acquaintances if pressed. "Why doesn't she tell Jim to take a hike? I mean, it's so obvious he wants to get in her pants and look at her—she's so closed off she might as well be an ice princess."

Paget glanced over her shoulder. "I'll give you the fact she's not open to his advances, but she's never going to tell him to buzz off. He's the vet for the ranch and she's one of the lead horse trainers. We end up working with Jim on a regular basis and with me taking a step back with my responsibilities, Annette and Cheyenne are relying on Heather more and more. She has to make nicey nice with Jim on a regular basis."

"She needs to do that when she's not punching the clock?"

"Sometimes. All the Whiskey siblings respect and value his opinion when it comes to the health of their animals. If he believes they aren't being treated right, and trust me, he's said things about ranch hands before, the Whiskey siblings listen." Paget lifted her index finger. "With a grain of salt. As a human, Jim might be weird, but he's a good vet and he's always willing to jump when we call. We need him."

"So, what you're telling me is she's just kissing ass."

"In some ways, she probably is, and in other ways, they have a weird friendship. They've been close for as long as I can remember."

Crew understood their bond, but he didn't understand what his eyes were seeing right now; however, he liked and respected Heather enough that he would at least ask her about Jim one more time.

"My husband is going to kill me because this is none of my business." Paget leaned forward. "This is a small town and people talk and lots of people are talking about you and Ashley, so if you want something with—"

"Whoa. Back that up a second. Me and Ashley?"

Paget nodded. "I was told she spent the night—"

"You were told wrong." Crew took his glass of water and chugged it. He should go back to Detroit. If anyone did spend the night at his place there, no one would care, much less talk about it.

"I didn't mean to offend you. But if I'm hearing

this, then Heather is hearing it too, which might explain the look on her face."

"No offense, but dating in a small town sucks." Crew tossed his napkin on the table. As soon as Boone reappeared, Crew needed to get Heather alone, even if for only a few moments. "May I ask you who told you they saw Ashley leaving my home?"

"Jim told me."

---

*H*eather had to be honest, if only with herself, that the only reason she'd come to Boone's was she'd been hoping that Crew would be having his usual dinner break and she'd have an opportunity to have a few stolen moments with him.

What she didn't expect was the weird sideways glances or that he'd spend half his time with Paget.

Of course, she was at a table with Jim, who she also wanted a chance to talk with.

Alone.

But so far, she hadn't been given the opportunity to ask her questions because every time she tried to talk to him, he had some excuse on why he couldn't separate himself from the crowd.

And Zuri and Fiona had joined them, making it even harder.

"What's going on with you?" Jim leaned across the table and whispered. "You're unusually quiet and distant."

She glared at him. "I've been trying to talk to you about what you said to me earlier today. I need to know what you meant about my co-workers."

Jim leaned against the high-top and looked around. "I overheard Carl and a few others talking that you've had your head in the clouds lately."

"That's ridiculous."

Jim nodded. "But Carl was specific about the horses and he came to me asking me to do a cluster on Alpine."

"What? Carl cleans the barn. He barely does anything with the horses. Why would he do that?"

"Well, Alpine was one of the horses sharing water with Izzy."

Heather opened her mouth, but Jim raised his hand. "I wasn't going to bother, but then I took a closer look and the feed in Alpine's stall was moldy and sure enough, the culture came back the same as Izzy's and Dixon's."

"Are you saying I'm poisoning the animals on Whiskey Ranch?"

Jim shook his head. "And that's not what Carl is saying, either."

"Really? Because that's what it sounds like from where I'm sitting."

"I agree with Heather," Fiona said. "Sounds like Carl is accusing her of some pretty nasty shit and I don't like it."

"Me neither." Zuri tapped her fingernails on the wood tabletop. "Heather wouldn't hurt a fly."

He reached across the table and took Heather's hand.

She shrugged it away.

"He's only concerned about the animals and he's afraid to say anything because he doesn't want to get you in trouble," Jim said. "He's been concerned about you for a while now."

"They why doesn't he come to me?" Heather took a good sip of wine. "Forget it. I'm going to confront Carl. First, I didn't do what he's saying, and second, I can't have this kind of tension at work."

Jim closed his eyes for a brief moment, letting out a slow breath. "If you have to, go ahead, but I'd prefer you leave me out of it."

"I'll do my best."

"Oh crap," Zuri said. "Look who just walked in."

Heather glanced over her shoulder.

She waved to Ashley, who took a quick scan around the room before pointing to herself.

Heather nodded.

"What are you doing now?" Jim asked.

She really had no idea what she was doing. In the past, she didn't give a shit what anyone thought. When she lost the baby and broke up with Shay, there were a million and one rumors, and she let them all fly without a second thought. Her life and pain were no one else's business.

But this? She couldn't let sit and she didn't understand why. "I want to know why she's telling people she saw me leave Crew's house this morning when—"

"It was actually her leaving my house," Crew's voice echoed off the walls.

Heather sloshed her drink. Red wine tumbled out of the glass, over her skin, and onto the table. "Shit. You scared me."

"Sorry. Paget and Boone just left and I wanted to come over and say hello to all of you and I heard your comment. However, I'm more curious as to why Jim is telling people Ashley spent the night."

Heather cocked her head, staring at Jim, whose gaze darted around the room, avoiding hers like a guilty kid.

Jim covered his mouth and coughed. "I said I saw

her at Crew's house before the sun came out; I never said she spent the night."

"What was Ashley doing at your house? Before sunrise?" Shit. She sounded like a jealous girlfriend. Not her intention, but she wanted to know the answer, nonetheless.

"She stopped by on her way to work to ask me some questions about a guy who has been stalking her," Crew said with a clipped attitude. "But here she comes, so ask her yourself."

"Ask me what?" Ashley smiled as she reached out and curled her fingers around his forearm.

"There seems to be some confusion as to who was at Crew's house this morning and why." Heather dug into her purse and pulled out a twenty, slamming it on the table. That should cover her glass of house wine during happy hour.

Ashley tilted her head and pursed her lips. "This is uncomfortable."

"Not really," Crew said. "It's a pretty simple and straightforward question, especially when some people in this town have misinterpreted your little visit this morning or chose to downright lie about it."

"Oh my." She covered her mouth as if she were embarrassed. "I'm sorry if what I repeated offended anyone."

"It's not that." Heather really didn't care, except the rumor had been used to make her look bad at the ranch when it came to the sick horses. That pissed her off and she wasn't going to take that sitting down. "I would just appreciate it if you didn't discuss my comings and goings with everyone in town."

"I don't think it's Ashley you should be upset with." Crew folded his arms and leaned against the high-top table. He stared at Jim, who shifted his weight from his left to his right and back again in an uncomfortable motion.

"Really? Then who?" Heather asked. "And why?"

"Let's start with this question." The corner of Crew's lips turned upward into an all-knowing smirk.

As if he were having a bit too much fun.

"Ashley, did someone suggest you come see me about those annoying texts?"

Ashley lifted her hand and bit down on her thumbnail. She glanced in Jim's direction.

That wasn't lost on Heather and she didn't need to be a detective to understand what that meant.

"I did tell her she should speak to someone." Jim set his glass on the table. "And I did suggest you."

"Did you also tell someone that you saw her leaving my place this morning?"

Jim planted his hands on his hips. "Are we in the second grade? Because that's what this feels like."

Crew laughed.

Now Heather was slightly lost. "What the hell is going on?"

"I want to know the answer to that too," Fiona said, looping her arm around Heather's shoulders.

"Small-town gossip bullshit and jealous games that I just don't have the time or patience for." Crew waved to the hostess who held up a to-go bag, setting it on the front station by the main door. "I don't know what everyone's deal is here, but I don't need to be the center of it." He tipped his head. "Have a nice evening."

Heather opened her mouth, but quickly snapped it shut.

What was she supposed to say? Besides, she wanted to know more about what the fuck just happened before she said anything else to him. She took a big sip of courage and then shook out her hands.

"Are you okay?" Zuri asked.

Heather nodded.

"I'm going to go—"

"You're not going anywhere," Heather interrupted Ashley. "Nor are you." She pointed to Jim. "Not until I know exactly what happened."

"What are you talking about?" Jim narrowed his gaze. "It's pretty obvious there was miscommunication and some gossip that resulted in people thinking Crew had multiple partners. The poor man."

If Heather were any other woman and Jim wasn't her friend, she'd pop him right in the nose. "Right. Because that makes him a stud and Ashley and me his sluts."

"Jesus, Heather. That's not what I mean, and you know it." Jim took a peanut from the basket and cracked it, sending the shell to the floor before popping the treat into his mouth.

"You're digging yourself a nice hole," Fiona said.

"Why would you tell anyone you saw me leaving his house?" Ashley asked. "Especially after you encouraged me to go talk to him?"

"What I want to know is why you'd say she spent the night." Zuri tossed a nut in his direction but missed wide right by a mile.

"I didn't say she spent the night." Jim let out a big puff of air. "And Ashley, why did you tell me that you saw Heather at Crew's place right before you got there, as in she's the one who spent the night."

"Oh no. I never said that." Ashley shook her head.

"Yes. You did."

"No. We talked about the fact they had dinner. That's all," Ashley said. "Why are you lying?"

"I'm not. You are and I have to wonder if those text messages, that you wouldn't show me but were so concerned about, are indeed real." Jim stiffened his spine and cocked his head as if he'd just won some battle.

Ashley gasped. "How dare you say such a thing to me." She tightened her purse over her shoulder, gripping it with both hands. "I'm not going to stand here and be spoken to like this." She stomped off into the crowd.

"That was a little harsh," Fiona said.

"Perhaps, but she flat out told me that she saw Heather leaving right before she pulled in. She absolutely made it sound like something happened. I feel like she set this whole thing in motion, only I don't understand why."

"Unless she wants Crew," Fiona said. "And I think every woman with a pulse in this town has a secret crush on the man."

"And why is that?" Jim asked. "Yes. I really want to know what he has that the rest of us regular Joes don't."

"He's mysterious," Fiona said.

"He's not from here," Zuri added. "And he has

that bad boy attitude, even though he's one of the good guys."

"And what do you see in him?" Jim asked.

"He's got an old soul," Heather admitted. "He's different from anyone I've ever met, but after tonight, I think whatever might have been brewing is no longer there."

"You're going to give up that easily?" Fiona asked.

"I'm not interested in games or trying to win someone over, and when this kind of shit happens, it's just too hard. I mean he stormed out in a mood over gossip, which in a way I can't blame him, but if that's how it's going to be after one date, no, thank you."

"Come on, that's being stupid. You should give him another chance."

This reminded her of when she lost the baby and she and Shay broke up. Everyone in town had an opinion and it made her crazy. And of course, because she hadn't wanted to share her other heartache, everyone kept telling her she could try again.

Only she couldn't.

She'd never have her own children.

Something she still struggled with fully accepting, and not because she wanted kids. Before she'd become pregnant, that had been a bone of contention with Shay and they often fought over when and if they'd ever have a family. She kept thinking someday in the future she'd want maybe one, where Shay wanted three or four and that always overwhelmed her, so they had settled on two, maybe in five years.

But it got to the point she didn't believe their relationship would last.

Then she peed on a stick and everything changed.

Now that the ability had been completely stripped of her and she couldn't even make that choice for herself, the idea of having a child became appealing.

Of course, having lost one also made her want something she couldn't have.

"Come on. Don't let Ashley and whatever little game she's playing ruin the start of something that could be really awesome between you and Crew," Fiona said. "You really like him and it shows."

"I can't believe I'm going to admit this." Jim pinched the bridge of his nose. "But I agree with Fiona. If you like the guy, you shouldn't let a little stupid gossip get in the way."

"That's mighty big of you." Zuri tapped her glass against Jim's. "Considering she basically rej—"

"You don't need to rub it in." Jim lowered his

chin. "Because I could make your life miserable at work."

"Good point." Zuri nodded.

"But all I want is for you to be happy," Jim said. "And if Crew could give you that, then you should go for it."

"I'm tired. It's been a long day." She pushed her twenty across the table. "I'll see you three tomorrow."

"I'll walk you to your car." Jim placed his hand on the small of her back.

She took a small step away, putting some space between them. She didn't mean to be rude, but her nerves were beyond frazzled and she didn't need any more gossip. "That's not necessary."

"I just want a word with you alone."

"Fine." This day would never end. She pushed through the door and inhaled the spring air. It smelled like freshly grilled beef mixed with warm cookies right from the oven. She pulled her keys out and unlocked her door. "What do you want?"

"To apologize. I realize my behavior hasn't been much better than that of a teenage boy and I'm sorry."

"It's okay. I just don't understand Ashley and why she'd tell you that."

He shrugged. "I really have no idea, but I

shouldn't have repeated it and honestly, the only reason I did was because I was trying to find out if it was really true or not."

"You could have asked me."

"That would be rude," he said. "And it's none of my business. You've made it quite clear where we stand."

She reached out and took his hand. "You've been a good friend. Thank you."

"Now, since you're not going to be dating Crew, how about—"

"Jim."

"I'm joking." He winked. "Drive safely. Call me if the horses aren't a hundred percent by morning."

She nodded, climbing in behind the steering wheel. Now she needed to talk with Crew and she wasn't about to do it in text messages, or wait until she ran into him at a later date.

No. She needed to clear the air now. That way, the next time they ran into each other there'd be no awkwardness and no one would look at them and wonder what the hell happened. She'd had enough of that after she and Shay broke up.

7

*C*rew stuffed his notepad in his back pocket, folded his arms across his chest, and leaned against his patrol car.

The domestic fight had resulted in a man with a gunshot wound to the gut.

It was hard to feel sorry for him when he'd given his wife a bloody nose, two black eyes, and a split lip.

For the eighth time.

"Hey," Shay jogged across the driveway. "I just got word Steven's sending over a patrol car to escort us to the ER. They are five minutes out."

"I'll wait until they get here."

"I appreciate that. I also wanted to thank you for helping to de-escalate the situation. She was going to shoot him again."

"Can you blame her?"

Shay shook his head. "She's never pressed charges. I know Steven's been out here a dozen times and has tried to get her to leave. So has her cousin, Fiona, but she won't and she's always defending him."

"She's related to Fiona? Heather's friend?"

Shay nodded, pointing to the car rolling to a stop down the road. "Speak of the devil." Shay waved. "I have to admit I was shocked when I'd heard it was her who pulled the trigger, and not him, and I'm sure Fiona is going to be doing the happy dance as well."

"My report, as will my testimony, if necessary, will say she did so in self-defense and hopefully that bastard will stay behind bars."

"At least we can get her away from him long enough to talk to her about how she can take the power back. I'm hoping you'll let her go home with Fiona tonight."

"No reason for her to spend the night in county lockup. The DA won't press charges against her, but he might go after her civilly, so I'd suggest she get a good lawyer, as well as a good therapist."

"It's so hard to break this cycle."

Crew nodded; however, his mind wandered to Heather. His anger over whatever game Ashley, and maybe Jim, had been playing had soured his mood so badly, he'd left Heather without saying goodbye and she hadn't reached out to him.

Not that he'd texted her in the last hour and a half, which he should. He owed her an apology. Not really the other way around. She hadn't done anything wrong, except get stuck in the middle of stupid gossip.

Why did he care what people thought anyway?

He was sure this wasn't the first time the good folks of Buhl, Idaho, brought his name up in casual conversation. But what irritated him was that they were gossiping about Heather and what she might be doing or not doing and that did bother him on a fundamental level.

"You look deep in thought," Shay said. "Is there something else about this scene that is troubling you?"

"No. Sorry. I just have a few things on my mind."

"A few things, or a good-looking brunette?"

"I hate small towns," Crew mumbled.

Shay chuckled. "You get used to it and when it comes to the big things, people don't talk about it so openly. Trust me on that."

"But everyone knows about it."

"That's where you're wrong." Shay turned and leaned against the patrol car. He ran his hand over his face. "I've lived here my entire life and it's comforting to know most people know and, more importantly, respect my history. There's still some chatter about it from time to time. Probably because I'm still single and so is Heather. But that's not because she and I have any real feelings left for one another."

"Why are you telling me this?"

"Because I know Heather and she tells the men she dates the part of our story that sounds like the hardest. The part that most people in this town don't know. The part that sends most good men running. Because that's what she wants to happen."

"No offense. But I don't think she'd appreciate you having this discussion with me."

"Of course she wouldn't. But Heather either hangs out with the likes of Jim, which I will never understand, or she dates men who want her to be something she's not, and that's always a recipe for disaster. If she's dated anyone for more than a few months, I'd be shocked."

"And she does this why?"

"I don't know." Shay shrugged. "I mean, I was one of those men, as in I wanted to change her. We lasted a lot longer, for a variety of reasons to which I won't bore you with the details because that would really piss her off if I did. But the bottom line is, I get the impression you don't like it when anyone molds their personality just to be with someone else."

"And here I thought you were an EMT and not a shrink."

Shay laughed. "I'm actually a certified emergency medical psychiatric technician, but I don't think you need a straitjacket. Yet."

"Gee, thanks." Crew glanced across the street.

Fiona had stopped to talk to her cousin, who, it appeared, kept trying to get to the ambulance, which meant she might be changing her mind already.

That happened a lot with victims.

Crew signaled to the beat cop. "Check on that," he said. "Make sure you keep them separate. We'll be rolling out in five."

The beat cop nodded.

"Before Fiona comes over and you really have to leave, can I ask you a couple of personal questions?"

"Sure," Shay said. "But I reserve the right to decline answering."

"Why did you bring up Heather?"

"Because she came to me for advice an hour ago and Heather and I don't talk often. As a matter of fact, the last time we talked about either of us having a relationship was a few months ago when she told me I was an asshole for the way I treat Fiona and then again an hour ago for the same thing."

"You and Fiona?"

"We have an arrangement. It doesn't work for either of us, but I can't seem to change the narrative. If you want the whole truth, most people believe I'm still hung up on Heather." Shay pushed from the car. "I'm not. I have no idea what Heather told you, but my problems with Fiona aren't because of Heather. However, they are because of something that happened when Heather and I were together."

"She told me."

"I doubt it," Shay said. "She probably told you about the miscarriage, or even how..." He paused and rubbed his eyes. "...that's not for me to say." Shay blew out a puff of air. "When Heather lost the baby, she was working at the ranch. No big deal. There was no reason why she shouldn't work. Only, I didn't want her to. I wanted her to be something she's not. A problem I have with Fiona, only I go at it from a different direction."

Crew really wanted to interrupt Shay, because he wasn't sure he wanted all the details.

Then again, if it helped him understand Heather, and why he couldn't get her out of his mind, he'd listen to the babble.

"When she felt something happening, she was on the trails. She radioed for someone to come out and finish the tour so she could go put her feet up and rest. She had no idea she was about to lose our kid. By the time she got halfway to the barn, she was bleeding pretty good. We'd had a fight that morning over stupid things and I chose not to take the call. Actually, I ignored five calls and eight texts, all begging me to come to the ranch." He wiped his face with a towel. "She did get ahold of 9-1-1 and Jim. But it was too late."

Crew stretched out his arm and squeezed Shay's shoulder. "There was nothing anyone could do to save your baby."

"I know that. The miscarriage was inevitable. But I was fifteen minutes away. EMTs were forty minutes, and Jim was clear across the ranch with only a golf cart. It took him twenty-five minutes to get to her. I could have saved her from having a hysterectomy, but instead, she nearly bled to death."

Jesus. "That's not your fault."

"Isn't it, though?"

Out of the corner of Crew's eye, he saw Fiona stroll down the driveway. There was more he wanted to say to this man. Crew understood taking on blame better than anyone and while he knew his drive to bring down a murderer led to the death of his wife and daughter, Darla, if she were still alive, would be the first one to say Crew did what he had to in order to ensure the safety of many.

She wasn't the first collateral death in one of his murder cases. It had happened before and it always broke his heart.

He just never expected it to happen so close to home. He always thought he'd be able to protect his family. To keep them safe from the darkness that was his career, but in an instant, his worlds collided, forever changing his future.

"We should talk more," Crew said. "I have my own tragedy that—"

"My cousin is with the eighty-third outside of Detroit. He's actually the captain."

"Shit. You're related to Captain Lawson?"

"He's actually my mom's cousin, but closer to my age. We're not all that close, but we went on a hunting trip two months ago. Oddly, your name came up and he told me what happened. I'm real sorry about your loss."

"Thanks."

"For the record, if it matters to you, people around here don't know and if they did, that's the kind of shit we don't talk about. Like I said, the big things, the things that really matter, we don't gossip about. But since you brought it up, I wanted you to know."

"I appreciate that."

"And I'd love to grab a beer with you sometime."

Shay stretched out his arm out toward Fiona. "Hey, babe," he said.

"I was hoping his wounds were so bad that you were letting him die out here," Fiona said.

"I was just about to take him to the hospital." Shay embraced Fiona. "We've got him this time."

"Only my cousin is being an idiot again." Fiona dropped her head to Shay's shoulder.

Crew leaned into his patrol car and pulled out his cell. He pulled up the contact information for a friend of his that dealt with abused women. He jotted the info on a piece of paper. "Here. Call this gal. She deals with people in this situation every day and she'll talk her into not only staying away, but making sure he pays."

"Thanks, Crew." Fiona took the paper.

"I have to go before I get fired." Shay kissed Fiona's forehead. "I'll see you in the morning. Call me if you need me."

Fiona folded the paper and tucked it in her purse. "I'm sorry about what happened earlier today at Boone's place. None of us can figure out why Ashley did what she did, and Jim knows he was wrong in trying to stir the pot. He's had a crush on her on and off for years."

"I know," Crew said. "I'm not used to the everyone-knows-everything in small towns and I might have overreacted a bit."

"Maybe a little," Fiona said, holding up her hands. "I better get going."

"Call my friend. And let me know how I can help."

"Thanks."

Crew glanced at his watch. All he wanted to do was take a hot shower, grab a bowl of cereal, and climb into bed with his dogs.

And maybe dream about Heather.

Maybe.

---

*H*eather couldn't stand listening to the dogs whine and scratch at the front door another second longer.

"I hear you," she said as she went searching for a key. Would a cop actually leave one out on the front porch?

Probably not, but she overturned every pot, chair, and anything that wasn't bolted down. What really surprised her was how little his dogs barked. Maybe it was because they knew her, or perhaps they were shitty watchdogs. They were pretty mellow when she'd been over before. Not once did they jump, nor did Crew have to yell at them. As a matter of fact, they were the most well-behaved dogs she'd ever come across, and that was saying something because King and Kong, JW's dogs, were pretty darn good.

"Well, no key here." She tugged at the door, just in case it was unlocked. No such luck. She ran her hand across the picture window and pushed.

Locked.

It had been nearly three hours since she'd left Boone's place. The department had told her that he was technically off duty an hour ago, so where the hell was he?

But the real question she should be concerned about was why did she need to speak to him tonight? She kept telling herself she had no plans on pursuing him anymore, so what did it matter at this point?

She made her way to the back of the house by the light of her cell phone, which turned out not to be as bright as she thought it would be. And Crew didn't have a well-lit yard. As a matter of fact, he didn't have any lights except for the one hanging over the garage and two in the front yard. Otherwise, his house was as dark as night.

Thankfully, the sky was filled with a bright moon and a ton of stars. Though, that really didn't light up the ground or the yard, and she wished she'd never left the front yard.

The sound of an engine roaring down the street caught her attention. She held her breath as the lights flashed in the yard. She raced to the side of the house, hugging the side and peering around the corner, but the car disappeared down the road. She let out a long sigh and checked the back door.

Locked.

She felt around the edges and smiled when she fingered a key.

Bingo.

Gently, she pushed it into the hole and turned the handle.

Daisy and Duke went nuts inside, barking and whining. They jumped on the door.

She laughed. That's not how the two behaved the other day and she enjoyed the fact that they were, indeed, normal dogs.

"Down," she commanded as she stepped inside and both dogs immediately did as she requested. "You two are unusual, that's for sure." She flicked on the light over the kitchen sink. "Let's get you two a treat."

Daisy yelped and Duke danced in a circle by the back pantry.

She rustled through the cupboards until she

found what she was looking for and gave both dogs a nice little tasty bone and filled their water bowls. Then she found herself a glass of wine. She should feel uncomfortable. Hell, she just broke into a cop's house and that was an arrestable offense. She should let Crew know she was there waiting. She turned, looking for her purse, and gasped as she stared at a man holding a gun.

But not just any man.

"Fuck, Heather. I almost shot you," Crew said as he lowered his arm and set his gun on the table.

"Didn't you see my car outside?"

"Yes. But the house was dark, there was no noise, and for all I knew you were in here facedown in your own blood."

"Oh. I suppose that makes sense." She planted her hands on her hips and stared at his dogs who had curled up under the table with their bones. "Duke and Daisy are useless as watchdogs."

"Tell me something I don't know."

"How did they not hear you?"

"They were too busy getting treats from you," he said. "And they are hard of hearing." He took down a glass and poured himself a very large glass of wine. "Daisy is almost completely deaf, and Duke can hear but he can't hear high tones."

"I had no idea."

"It's one of the reasons they are so well behaved." He set his drink down on the table, ran a hand over his head, and pulled her into his arms. "Anyone ever tell you that breaking and entering is illegal?"

"I've heard that rumor." She rested her hands on his shoulders. She should really pull away, but she couldn't. Or wouldn't. Something about Crew made him irresistible.

But she really needed to talk with him about a few things and snuggling with him wasn't the way to go about that, no matter how wonderful it felt.

She patted his chest and stepped back. "I'm sorry I invaded your space."

"Other than I could have killed you, I'm not complaining."

"I think we need to talk."

"I don't disagree." He took his drink, laced his fingers through hers, and led her into the family room. "Ladies first."

"I'm not even sure I know where to start." She sat on the edge of the sofa, kicking off her shoes and tucking her feet under her butt. She stared at him, sipping her drink and feeling like a teenage girl waiting to get kissed for the first time. Her stomach was all in knots and her palms were all sweaty.

"I know I should start with an apology. I was rude to you earlier when you didn't deserve it."

"We got stuck in the middle of small-town gossip, which happens around here, but that was unusually weird and awkward." Heather stretched out her legs, letting her feet land on his thighs. "After you left, I found out that it was Ashley who told Jim she saw me leaving your place bright and early."

"Well, we both know she's lying." Crew gently massaged her ankle and calf muscles. "Did you find out why?"

"No. And I honestly don't care other than I don't understand what she gets out of starting a rumor like that, and when I left the bar, Jim was pretty upset—actually more like embarrassed—for repeating her rumor."

"Why did he?"

"Do you really have to ask that question?"

Crew shook his head. "I've always struggled with people knowing my business, but what's worse is people thinking they know and making judgments based on false information and that pissed me off. I don't know Ashley well and couldn't even make a reasonable assessment on why she did what she did, but Jim? He knew repeating it would add fuel to the fire."

"He did," she admitted. "He was jealous and he's not happy with himself."

"I know you and Jim have a long history and I

can respect that. But I get the impression there is more to that story than him being there for you when you lost your baby."

She took a long slow sip of wine and stared at the ceiling. If she answered the question, she broke the confidence she had with Jim.

If she didn't, she potentially ruined any chance she had with Crew.

"There is."

Crew leaned forward, taking her wine from her hands and setting it down on the coffee table. "I appreciate your honesty and for the record, I don't expect you to tell me what that is."

"I wish I could, but it's not for me to tell."

"I can understand that."

"It has to do with—"

He pressed his fingers against her lips. "I don't need you to tell me whatever it is that bonds you and Jim together. I just need to know that it's not romantic."

She palmed Crew's cheek. "Far from it."

"Shall we move your car into the garage or give this town something to talk about?"

"Why, Detective Irvin, are you propositioning me?"

He waggled his brow. "Are you going to turn me down?"

Butterflies filled her stomach. Her skin heated. All she could think about was racing to his bedroom and climbing under the covers. She hadn't been this excited about doing the nasty with a man since she'd been with Shay.

The anticipation of what it might be like with Crew tickled her senses. She'd thought about it many times in the privacy of her own bedroom, but never once expected she'd have the pleasure.

She curled her fingers around the hem of her shirt and tugged it over her head, tossing it to the side.

"I guess we're giving them something to gossip about at the water cooler." He tightened his grip on her thigh, staring at her chest as she reached behind her back and unclasped her bra, letting it fall to her lap.

She didn't have large breasts, but no one would describe them as tiny either.

Her nipples tightened in the air-conditioning, which in turn sent a warm shiver to her girly parts.

He licked his lips. His gaze darting from her eyes to her chest. His hands roamed up her body, cupping the soft swell of her breast. He ran his thumb over her tight nipple.

She arched her back and moaned.

His touch was firm, but soft. Gentle, yet rough. A contrast of sensations that sent her on a tailspin.

She clutched his head as he sucked on each nipple, staring down at him while he licked and nibbled. His stubble scratched at her skin, making her desperate for him. She reached for the buttons on her jeans and wiggled.

He lifted his head and smiled. "Let me help you with that." He lowered himself, kissing his way down her stomach, tugging her pants over her hips and down to her ankles before he pulled them right off. "So beautiful," he whispered as he slipped his fingers inside her, stroking gently, but firmly.

She spread her legs, begging for more. She hadn't been this selfish sexually in a long time.

If ever.

Except for maybe with Shay, sex had been a chore. It had been a means to an end. Something she did because it felt good and it gave her release.

There were times she found raw animal sex, which she craved, but those moments were few and far between and she never knew how to hold on to it when she found it mostly because there wasn't a man who gave her both the sex and the emotion.

It was always one or the other.

It was never both.

And she was okay with that because she realized she didn't want both from one man.

However, with Crew, she knew it would be the best of all worlds.

And that scared the fuck out of her.

She could handle great sex, but she wasn't sure she could handle the rest of it.

Crew dipped his head between her legs. His tongue and fingers worked in unison to bring her the kind of pleasure she'd only fantasized about.

"Oh, God." She draped her legs over his shoulders and dug her heels into his back. Heaving in a deep breath, she held it for a few seconds and then let it out with a groan. "Yes." Glancing down at him, she caught his gaze, and an orgasm took hold of her middle so tight it shocked her system. "Crew," she said with a shaky voice.

He stood, ripping off his shirt. He reached into his back pocket, yanked out his wallet, and presented a condom.

"I can't get pregnant."

"There are other things we should be concerned about."

"I haven't been with anyone in seven months."

He tossed the birth control pack over his shoulder. "A little longer for me." He lowered his pants.

She swallowed. "Oh my." She took him into her

hands, running her thumb over the tip and cupping him at the base. This had never been something she'd sought during the act of love, but right now, all she wanted was to explore his body. To find out what made him hiss.

And that didn't take too long when she brought him to her lips and took him into her mouth. His skin was soft, like silk. But he was harder than anything she'd ever touched before. It made her entire body burn. Everything exploded as if she were on fire. She was desperate to please him as she frantically licked and squeezed and stroked, wanting to hear and feel his orgasm ripple across his body.

"Heather," he said. "I need you to stop."

She blinked, staring up at him, holding him in her hands. "Why?"

"Because I want so badly to be inside you."

She smiled. "Okay."

He climbed onto the sofa and entered her in one quick, powerful thrust.

"Oh, God, Crew." She clutched his shoulders. "Please. Now."

He kissed her. Hard.

She wrapped her arms and legs around him, drawing him as deep inside as she could. She ground her hips against him as fast and as hard as her body would allow until her orgasm unleashed on the both of them. "Crew," she managed with a raspy breath.

He collapsed on top of her, finding a blanket and covering their bodies. He planted sweet, wet kisses on her neck while he breathed deeply. "Sweet Heather," he whispered.

She ran her fingers up and down his back. The sound of a car whizzing past reminded her that her vehicle was parked right out front. "If I'm going to spend the night, we probably should move my car."

"I gave you the option to move it before we got naked."

"We still have to go upstairs, because I'm not sleeping on this sofa, and there are two dogs staring at us right now. I'm assuming they need to go out, which means one of us is getting dressed. And that won't be me."

"So, this is how this relationship is going to be."

She laughed. "Is that what we're in?"

"We'll find out in the morning when the town starts talking about us."

8

*H*eather pulled into her parking spot at the main administration building at the ranch and ran a hand over her face, trying to wipe the smile away. Her cheeks hurt. She swore she must have been grinning while she slept. She glanced at her watch. She wasn't late, but she wasn't early either. She didn't normally work on the weekends, but the showcase was different, and she'd been pulling long hours between the sick animals and preparing for this event.

However, glancing around the parking lot, she suspected she was the last one to arrive.

That might be the last time Crew got a quickie in the shower.

Her smile returned bigger than ever.

She stepped from her vehicle, tossing her purse

over her shoulder, and waved to Cheyenne, who was coming down the hill in one of the ranch golf carts.

Only she didn't smile when she waved back.

"Good morning." Heather couldn't tell if the sour look on Cheyenne's face was due to pregnancy issues or something else.

"I wish I could say it was."

That didn't sound good on any front. "What's wrong?"

Cheyenne jerked the cart to a stop and jumped from behind the steering wheel. "This." She shoved some papers at Heather. "What the hell is going on with you?"

"Excuse me?" In all the years Heather has worked at Whiskey Ranch, no one has ever spoken to her like that. She took the documents and scanned them, noting the feed company and the dates. "I canceled this order and told Carl that if they showed this morning not to accept it."

"That's not what happened and not what Carl said and now we've got a couple more sick animals and a horse that probably won't make it."

"What? Who?"

"Alpine," Cheyenne said.

"That's impossible. When I left yesterday..." She let her words trail off as she flipped the page and glossed over the ranch after-hours sign-in sheet. Her name scribbled in black ink jumped out at her. "I never follow protocol if I come back at night. You know that. None of us trainers do."

"So, why is your name there?" Cheyenne flicked the stack of papers. "And JD is inside pulling past night shift documents, and he texted to tell me that your name is on a few other ones." Cheyenne let out a long breath. "All nights where something happened to one of the horses."

Heather blinked. "This is crazy." She handed the pages back to Cheyenne. "First. I would never hurt an animal. Second. What would be the motive? And finally, why on earth would I all of a sudden start leaving a signature behind when since I was promoted to trainer and manager, I've never once signed in after hours? Though, I'm thinking maybe we need to have that become a policy for everyone." She planted her hands on her hips. "I can't believe you'd even think that for one—"

"I don't think that. None of us do. But the evidence is kind of damning and Alpine is suffering bad. Jim is with him now; however, he's going to have to put him down and there are other horses sick again. And the worst part is all the feed that was accepted by this vendor, that has been proven to be bad in the past, is missing and this shows you signed for it."

"Does it say what time?"

Cheyenne nodded. "Four-thirty in the morning."

Heather shook her head. "I was snug as a bug in a rug in bed."

"Alone?"

"Are you seriously asking me that? You really think I'd do this?" Heather asked.

"No. I'm just trying to..." Cheyenne raised her palms to the air. "I don't know. It's been a hell of a confusing morning and I just wish I could say fuck you to the world, my girl Heather didn't do this."

"Well. I didn't. And I can prove it, but I'm not sure my bed partner would appreciate me tossing him under the bus."

"Crew?"

Heather nodded.

Cheyenne cocked her head and arched a brow. "Interesting alibi. Half the people who work here would have driven by his place. I guess they would have seen your car."

"First, I can't believe you said that and second, no. It was in his garage. You know how I feel about gossips and he has the same affliction."

"I said it because I believe you, and I need everyone else to as well." Cheyenne pointed toward the administration building.

JD stepped from the door and strolled down the path.

"He's been trying to find ways to prove to everyone on this ranch you couldn't have done any of what Carl and some of the other peons are basically accusing you of, but it's hard when there is also surveillance footage of a woman wearing dark clothing, with long dark hair, driving a ranch golf cart into the barn and turning off the security."

Heather leaned against her car. "Why didn't you call me? I would have come in earlier."

"At first we all thought you were here, in part because Carl said he saw you, which makes sense since he's the night shift. He said he thought you went down to the south barn to see if any horses were sick down there."

"When was that?"

"Two hours ago," Cheyenne said, holding up her hand. "The longer we couldn't find you on the ranch, the more we started to wonder if—"

"Wonderful. Just fucking wonderful. I believe you thought I'd—"

JD appeared at Cheyenne's side. "We thought someone hurt you and we called the police." He plopped a toothpick into his mouth. "Crew is up at the barn as we speak. He arrived about ten minutes ago. He told you to hang tight and he'd be right down."

"I want to go see Alpine before Jim puts him down." Heather took a strand of hair and twisted it between her fingers. She stared up the hill at the north barn in the distance. Crew's Jeep kicked up dirt as he came down the access road.

"It's probably too late for that," JD said. "I gave him the go-ahead a half hour ago. It would have been cruel to let that horse take another breath he was in so much pain."

Heather groaned. "I get the feeling someone has it out for me."

"I'm in agreement," JD said. "And I'm thinking Carl has something to do with it, but I can't figure out why. He's worked for us for the last five years and his record is solid. Did something happen between the two of you?"

"No. But he's been a bit standoffish with me," Heather admitted.

"He's been quiet lately." Cheyenne rested her hand on her growing belly.

Crew's Jeep jerked to a stop. He didn't bother turning the engine off. His cowboy boots hit the hard ground, stirring up the dirt. He tossed his Stetson to the passenger seat and pushed his sunglasses to the top of his head. He stretched out his arm and squeezed her shoulder. "Hey, Heather."

"Hi, Crew," she said, not really sure how this part of their relationship was going to work. They'd joked about going with the flow, but when the sun came up, they both realized, while they didn't care who knew, they just preferred not to announce it.

"I'm real sorry to hear about one of the horses. I know how much you care for them on the ranch."

"Thanks." She nodded.

"I emailed you copies of all the paperwork and videos you asked for," JD said.

"I appreciate it." Crew planted his hands on his hips and glanced around. "I take it JD has filled you in on the accusations."

"For the record, I don't care what my other employee is saying about Heather; I know there's no way she could have done any of this."

Crew caught her gaze. "I've gone through the timeline, according to the main eyewitness, and I know for a fact Heather couldn't have been on this property when Carl said she was. I also know for a fact that wasn't her on the surveillance footage."

Heather's heart swelled. Her pulse pounded in her throat. She felt like she was sixteen and waiting to be picked up for her first dance.

"Do you mind if I ask how you know this all to be one hundred percent true?" JD asked.

"Because she has a rock-solid alibi, only I'm not sure I want to toss it out there just yet."

"Why not?" She glared at him. "Not that I want my personal life out there for everyone to judge, but I don't like being accused of killing a horse or any of these other things. I'd kind of like to put an end to that and have the real culprit arrested."

"I'm with her," JD said.

"That's just it. I don't believe there is any way Carl acted alone and from what I've gathered, and what all of you have told me so far, I don't have a single suspect, other than Heather."

"I couldn't have done those things and you know it."

He nodded. "JD, can I have a moment with Heather?"

"Sure. I'll be in my office."

Crew curled his fingers around her forearm and walked her around the front of his Jeep. "I know it's going to be really shitty to have people think you could have done this, but if no one knows you were with me last night, whoever is helping Carl set you up will want to put the nail in your coffin, so to speak."

"Oh, because this isn't bad enough."

"It's really not bad enough for me to arrest you."

She narrowed her stare. "Because I was with you last night."

"Even if you weren't with me, or had a really good alibi, there isn't enough evidence to arrest you on anything. A horse eating bad feed doesn't equal the murder or abuse of a horse. Right now, all Carl has done has set up the idea you're not good at your job."

"Oh, jeez, thanks. You really know how to make a girl feel really good about herself."

"Look. So far this morning, I've been at the gym, the coffee shop, and now here. Not a single person has looked at me funny or said a thing about you being at my place last night. Anyone say anything to you?"

"Cheyenne knows, but not from gossip."

"All right. But will she tell anyone? Because, seriously, if I'm going to find out who is doing this, I need them to think I'm not really good at my job and that you're the prime suspect."

"Can my life get any weirder?"

He nodded. "I don't want you to be alone. Today is technically my day off and when I'm done here, it's going to look as if I believe you might be a suspect."

"I'm not liking you very much right now."

"Trust me. I'm not high on my list either," he said.

"Anyway, I'm going to go get my dogs and meet you back at your place, where I'm going to stay until all this is over."

"And how is that going to look to the world?"

"No one is going to know I'm there."

"How is that possible?"

"Because I'm really good at my job," he said. "All I need is a little time to figure out this guy's end game, set him up to make a mistake, and your reputation will be restored, and we can go back to sneaking around like a normal couple."

"There is nothing normal about us."

9

"*A*re you going to arrest her?" Carl asked, staring at Crew with pleading eyes.

Crew really wanted to know why Carl had such desperation in his gaze. This wasn't his ranch. It wasn't his horse. And yet, he was the only one calling for Heather to be taken away in handcuffs.

"You didn't actually see Heather sign for the feed, correct?"

"No. But she was the only manager signed onto the ranch. When there's a supervisor, that's the only person who can accept that kind of delivery."

"Does she always sign in that early?"

"Actually, no. I did think that was weird." Carl glanced over one shoulder and then the other. "But she's been doing some really weird shit for a while now and the night staff has been covering up for her and we just can't do it anymore."

"So, this isn't the first time her actions have resulted in the death of an animal?"

"Well. No. It is the first time for that, but horses have been hurt or gotten sick because of things Heather has done."

"Let me ask this." Crew flipped a page in his notebook. "Why do you believe she'd want to hurt the horses she trains and proclaims to love?"

"I don't know. Attention? Money? Maybe someone is paying her to sabotage the Whiskey family. That's happened before." Carl shook his head and shrugged his shoulders.

"That's an interesting theory." And one that Crew had every intention of looking into because that made perfect sense when it came to Carl. "Anything else I should know?"

"I can't think of anything else."

Crew took out one of his business cards. "If you think of anything, let me know."

"I sure will. Thanks."

Crew stuffed his notebook into his pocket and strolled down the path between the main corral and where he'd parked his Jeep. About the only thing he found out was that everyone on Whiskey Ranch struggled to believe that Heather could do such a thing.

The problem was in the idea they weren't opposed to the concept, based on the evidence and the way Carl presented what he saw, heard, and thought happened.

Only Carl was lying and Crew knew it. And Carl was painting a picture that was too neat. Too clean. He wasn't coloring outside of the lines; however, his story didn't fit.

"Hey. Crew. Wait up," a familiar voice shouted.

Crew glanced over his shoulder.

Jim.

"What's up?" Crew didn't stop; he just slowed to a snail's pace. He'd interviewed Jim when he first arrived and he didn't need to do it again.

"You're making a big mistake."

"Regarding?"

"Investigating Heather. Whatever happened, she didn't do it. Or if she did something that resulted in that animal being sick, it wasn't done on purpose."

For good measure, Crew pulled out his notebook, but he sure as hell wasn't going to write this down. "So, you believe she signed for an order that she and the owners of the ranch all say they canceled and told the delivery crew to reject?"

"I don't know who signed for it, but if Heather says she didn't, then she didn't."

"I have a security video that says otherwise."

Jim's eyes widened. He hadn't been on the list of people who'd seen the security footage, which Crew had been glad had been kept to a minimum.

"I don't believe it."

"Then give me a reason Carl would lie. A compelling one, because without that, the evidence against Heather is stacking up pretty high."

Jim stepped in front of Crew and stopped. He planted his hands on his hips. "This might be grasping because it would make more sense if he were trying to hurt me, but Carl is my ex-fiancée's cousin."

Crew did write that in his handy little notebook. "What was her name?"

"Bethany."

"And it would make more sense because she's a woman scorned? What is it that they would be getting back at you for?"

"Calling off the wedding."

"I thought she left you." Fuck. Now he was the one who was gossiping.

"It's a complicated story and one that people in this town only think they know the truth. But

Bethany would have married me even after I found out she was in love with someone else."

Crew cocked his head. "And who was that and why is it important to what is happening now?"

"Bethany is a closet lesbian."

"A closet what?"

Jim took out a handkerchief and ran it over his brow. "I swore I'd never tell anyone. In part because Bethany asked me not to and because I'm embarrassed that I didn't know the woman I'd fallen in love with preferred women over men."

"I see." Now that would suck. "But I'm not following how this has anything to do with what is going on here now."

"Bethany was in love with Heather."

"Well, now that does change my perspective on things," Crew said. "Where is Bethany now?"

"I have no idea. I'm going to assume she's up in Boise with her family."

"What about Ashley? Weren't they best friends?"

Jim let out a short laugh. "Ashley wasn't happy when she found out Bethany was gay and still wanted to marry me. She didn't understand why Bethany would want to keep it a secret."

"Why does she?"

"Her father's the head of a controversial conservative church that is totally in the dark ages, but she wouldn't bring shame on him that way. It's truly a sad dynamic."

"The gossip mills around this town don't paint that picture," Crew said.

"I'm aware. But until now, I've seen no reason to tell this story."

"I appreciate you coming forward with this information. If you wouldn't mind sending me any contact information for Bethany that you think might be helpful, I would appreciate it."

"Will do," Jim said.

"And if you hear from her, I want to know about it."

Jim nodded.

Crew stuffed his hands in his pockets and headed back down the path toward his Jeep, his mind churning the new information over, mixing it with everything else and he drew one single conclusion.

Heather was being set up and by an unlikely adversary.

---

*H*eather leaned against the tree trunk and tilted her head toward the star-filled sky. "You know, a stakeout doesn't count as a date."

Crew laughed, setting his binoculars on his lap.

"Hopefully, if my theory is correct, which I think it is, I'll have this case wrapped up by morning."

"I can't believe Jim told you about Bethany."

"He had to, for your sake." Crew snagged a water bottle and took a swig before shifting in front of the tree, leaning forward as if to be ready to jump into action. "I find it so weird that everyone in this town will gossip about anything and yet will keep a secret if asked."

Heather let out a slow breath. "That's true anywhere. It's human nature to do a little bit of both. But Bethany was so distraught over Jim calling off the wedding over something that didn't happen, and she went crazy."

Crew turned. "Crazy how?"

"I guess Jim didn't tell you everything." She reached out and rubbed Crew's shoulders. "Normally, I'd say you'd have to go to the source, but I think under the circumstances I can tell you."

"I wish you would. It would make it easier for me to protect you."

"Bethany came to me to tell me how she felt, expecting she and I could have an affair while she's married to Jim."

Crew chuckled. "I'm sorry. I shouldn't be laughing. But this is a bad made-for-television movie."

"Oh. I know. You can't make this shit up,"

Heather said. "Basically, I told her no and I begged her to tell Jim."

"I take it that didn't go over well."

"She told me she wouldn't tell him because she still planned on marrying him because that's what her father expected. Her father's church demanded it of her."

"I did do a little research and her father's religion is a cult and it's fucked up."

Heather nodded. "Anyway, I don't normally meddle, but I felt I couldn't look Jim in the eye day in and day out if I didn't say something. He called off the wedding and she went ballistic, saying we ruined her life and there would be consequences. A few weeks later, she was gone, and I haven't heard from her since."

"Looks like she's making good on her threats," Crew said. "I haven't really figured out how Ashley fits in. Jim said she was angry with Bethany for wanting to still marry him."

"I honestly didn't know Ashley knew anything. She and I aren't close. But it doesn't surprise me if she did," she said. "What exactly are we doing? I mean, what do you plan on finding out up here tonight?"

"If my little breadcrumbs worked, whoever is setting you up will be here."

"How can you be so sure?"

"Because they will want to seal your fate and be done with it and I'm giving them the opportunity," Crew said.

"And exactly how are you doing that?"

"All the players believe I think you're guilty as sin."

"That just makes me feel all warm and fuzzy." She swallowed the thick lump in her throat.

"If they think all I need is a little more evidence to pull the trigger and arrest you, they will do it as soon as possible and the fact that you were pulled off the showcase and everyone right now thinks you might be guilty, well, they are going to want to strike while the iron is hot."

She dropped her hands to her lap and narrowed her gaze, straining to see through the darkness.

A slender body slinked across the ground by the west side of the barn.

"Do you see that?" she whispered.

"I do," he said.

"Are you going to go slap some handcuffs on whoever that is?"

"All in good time." Slowly, Crew stood, offering a hand. "We need to catch them planting evidence to make this work." Crew pulled out his cell and tapped on the screen.

She inched closer to the fence. "I can't see."

"Here." Crew lifted his cell. "You can watch on the app with me."

"What?"

"JD and his family let me put in my own surveillance equipment." He held his phone in front of them.

The person—it was obvious the intruder was indeed a woman—set a large bag on the floor in the middle of the barn. She pulled out some medical supplies and a syringe big enough for a horse.

"No. No. I'm not going to stand here and watch her inject something into a horse. I won't." She took two steps forward.

Crew grabbed her arm. "You won't have to. Patience."

"Screw that." She tapped her finger aggressively on the screen, staring at Bethany holding a very large needle. "She's about to stick that in Dixon's body. I can't let her do that."

"And you won't." Crew hit a few icons inside the app.

A humming noise filled the air.

Lights illuminated the skies as a loud click echoed in her ears.

"Freeze. Put your hands in the air," Steven's voice boomed in the night.

"I wish we had some popcorn." Crew tossed his arm over her shoulders. "And better seats."

She snatched the cell and glanced between the tiny screen and what was unfolding about a football field away. Steven and a few other police officers had surrounded Bethany, who had dropped the needle and put her hands on top of her head.

"Is this going to be enough?"

"We have footage of Carl leaving the east service gate open, and somehow Bethany had a key to the main administration building, and we now have pictures of her entering and signing you in." Crew kissed her cheek. "We got her. It's over. And I don't have to do the paperwork." He pulled her into his arms. "Now, since my dogs are at your place, my only question is, do I need to park in your garage, or are we going to really give this town something to talk about?"

A smile tugged at the corners of her mouth as she wrapped her arms around Crew's strong and comforting body. She didn't know what her future would hold, but she hoped that Crew would be a part of it.

"You can leave the car outside on one condition."

"What's that?"

"You make me some apple cobbler for breakfast."

EPILOGUE
THREE MONTHS LATER...

*C*rew tossed his keys on the table by the front door in the foyer. Daisy and Duke greeted him with a quick hello before racing off to wherever Heather was, because they seemed to become more attached to her than him.

Figures.

"Honey, I'm home," he said in his best Cuban accident. Things had moved pretty quickly in the last couple of months and that both excited and scared him, but he loved Heather and he couldn't deny that one second longer.

He was tired of spending a night here and then dragging the dogs over to her place. He wanted a home again and he wanted it with Heather.

"Hey, babe, I'm in the kitchen."

"That's kind of scary." He strolled through the

hallway, pausing at one of the pictures. Another change he needed to make. He ran a finger over the one of him, Gypsy, and Darla that had been taken about a month before the murders. He lifted the frame off the wall. Being with Heather didn't change how much he missed them. It didn't fill the void in his soul or even ease the pain.

It did change his existence and gave him a reason to live. Loving Heather gave him purpose and helped him honor those he'd lost.

"There you...oh." Heather reached out and squeezed his biceps. "I think that's one of my favorite pictures of all of you."

"How do you do it?"

"Do what?" Heather asked.

"Come over here all the time and not beg me to take all these pictures down?"

"The same reason you'd never ask me to get rid of the box of reminders I have in my closet."

He opened his mouth, but she pressed her finger over his lips. "I know you've seen it and I know you've opened it."

"I didn't mean to invade your privacy."

"I know. But I'm surprised you've never suggested, like the rest of my family, how unhealthy it is to keep a pregnancy test, the hospital bracelets from when I lost the baby, even the bloody outfit I was wearing, but in a strange way, it's comforting."

"I understand why you've kept it and if and when you're ready to purge, I'll be there with you. However, this has become overkill. It's a shrine and while I'll always want a couple of pictures of them on display, the majority of them need to go into storage." He hung the picture back on the wall and took her by the hand, leading her to the sofa. "We need to talk."

"I don't like the sound of that."

He held her gaze and sucked in a deep breath. "We've said from the beginning we're two broken souls keeping it casual, but I don't want to do that anymore."

She cocked her head. "What do you mean?"

"I'm in love with you, Heather, and I want us to be together. To live together. I was thinking we could buy that place on the other side of town and start fresh."

She gasped and jerked to a standing position. She paced in front of the fireplace, twisting her hair.

"That's not the response I had expected. I was hoping you might say you loved me back."

She paused, staring at him with an unblinking gaze, like a doe in headlights. "Oh. Crew. I do. I do love you. With all my heart."

He stood.

She held up her hand. "But—"

"Don't say but."

"We need to address the elephant in the room." Tears rolled down her cheeks.

"I don't see one." He had no idea what in the hell she was talking about. "What's wrong? I don't understand."

She raced to the wall of images and pulled down the picture of Gypsy the day they took her home. "I can't give you this. I can't give you a family."

"Is that what this is about?" He took the picture from her hands. His heart swelled. He remembered the day like it was yesterday.

"Of course it is. Eventually, this has to end because you're going to see how much you really want a family and—"

"Do you want one?"

"I can't have one." She pursed her lips and swiped at her cheeks.

"That's not what I asked."

"It doesn't matter if I want one or not."

"Oh, sweetheart, but it does." He held up the picture. "This is the day we took Gypsy home."

Heather gasped. "Why are you telling me this? It's not helping. It's actually cruel. You can go on to have a family again."

"So can you."

She raised her palms toward the ceiling and slapped them to her thighs. "Why are you being so mean?"

"It was the day *we* took her to our home. Not home from the hospital." He pushed the image in front of her face. "Does that look like a baby that was only a couple of days old?"

She glanced between him and the photograph. "Well. No."

"That's because when we got Gypsy, she was three months old. We had waited months—no—almost two years to adopt a baby."

"I didn't know that," Heather said quietly.

"I'm sorry. I should have told you sooner. I guess I thought you somehow knew." Crew raked his hand through his hair. "We've never talked about our future, and I want to change that because I want one with you."

"I need to sit down." She patted down the sofa until she found the spot she wanted. "I never brought it up because I figured one of us would get bored and move on."

"You just said you loved me, so you thought I'd be the one to tire of this."

She nodded.

"I could never be bored with you." Joining her on

the sofa, he took her chin with his thumb and fore-finger. "Do you want to have a family? Because carrying a child yourself isn't the only way to make that happen."

"You loved Gypsy like she was you—"

He pressed his finger over her lips. "I've always hated it when people said that I loved her like my own. She was my daughter. Just because Darla and I didn't make her, didn't mean we weren't her parents."

Heather palmed his cheek. "You are the most amazing man I've ever known, and I don't know how I got so lucky."

"And you still haven't answered my question."

"I love you," she said. "And I want to move in with you and I want to continue this discussion."

He kissed her palm. "How about we go upstairs, have a little quickie, and then head off to Boone's for a celebratory dinner and tell everyone we're getting married."

"What? When did we go from living together to getting married?"

"When we decided to give this town something to talk about."

Thank you for reading *Whiskey Cobbler*.

Please feel free to leave an HONEST review.
Next up is *Whiskey Smash!* Get you copy today!

*Sign up for my Newsletter (https://dl.bookfunnel.com/
6atcf7g1be) where I often give away free books before
publication.*

*Join my private Facebook group (https://www.facebook.
com/groups/191706547909047/) where I post exclusive
excerpts and discuss all things murder and love!*

Never miss a new release. Follow me on
Amazon:amazon.com/author/jentalty
And on Bookbub: bookbub.com/authors/jen-talty

Jen Talty is the *USA Today* Bestselling Author of Contemporary Romance, Romantic Suspense, and Paranormal Romance. In the fall of 2020, her short story was selected and featured in a 1001 Dark Nights Anthology. She is currently contracted to write in the *With Me in Seattle* series by Kristen Proby with Lady Boss Press, as well as Susan Stoker's *Special Forces: Operation Alpha* and Elle James's *Brotherhood Protectors.*

Regardless of the genre, her goal is to take you on a ride that will leave you floating under the sun with warmth in your heart. She writes stories about broken heroes and heroines who aren't necessarily looking for romance, but in the end, they find the kind of love books are written about :).

She first started writing while carting her kids to one hockey rink after the other, averaging 170 games per year between 3 kids in 2 countries and 5 states. Her first book, IN TWO WEEKS was originally published in 2007. In 2010 she helped form a publishing company (Cool Gus Publishing) with *NY Times* Bestselling Author Bob Mayer where she ran the technical side of the business through 2016.

Jen is currently enjoying the next phase of her life... the empty nester! She and her husband reside in Jupiter, Florida.

Grab a glass of vino, kick back, relax, and let the romance roll in...

Sign up for my Newsletter (https://dl.bookfunnel. com/6atcf7g1be) where I often give away free books before publication.

Join my private Facebook group (https://www.facebook. com/groups/191706547909047/) where I post exclusive excerpts and discuss all things murder and love!

Never miss a new release. Follow me on Amazon:amazon.com/author/jentalty

And on Bookbub: bookbub.com/authors/jen-talty

ALSO BY JEN TALTY

Club Temptation

SWEET TEMPTATION

Legacy Series

DARK LEGACY

With Me In Seattle

INVESTIGATE WITH ME

SAIL WITH ME

The Monroes

COLOR ME YOURS

COLOR ME SMART

COLOR ME FREE

COLOR ME LUCKY

COLOR ME ICE

It's all in the Whiskey

JOHNNIE WALKER

GEORGIA MOON

JACK DANIELS

JIM BEAM

WHISKEY SOUR

WHISKEY COBBLER

WHISKEY SMASH

Search and Rescue

PROTECTING AINSLEY

PROTECTING CLOVER

PROTECTING OLYMPIA

PROTECTING FREEDOM

PROTECTING PRINCESS

NY State Trooper Series

IN TWO WEEKS

DARK WATER

DEADLY SECRETS

MURDER IN PARADISE BAY

TO PROTECT HIS OWN

DEADLY SEDUCTION

WHEN A STRANGER CALLS

NY State Trooper Novella

HIS DEADLY PAST

THE CORKSCREW KILLER

THE LOST SISTER

THE LOST SOLDIER

THE LOST SOUL

THE LOST CONNECTION

A Spin-Off Series: Witches Academy Series

THE NEW ORDER

Special Forces Operation Alpha

BURNING DESIRE

BURNING KISS

BURNING SKIES

BURNING LIES

BURNING HEART

BURNING BED

REMEMBER ME ALWAYS

The Brotherhood Protectors

Out of the Wild

ROUGH JUSTICE

ROUGH AROUND THE EDGES

ROUGH RIDE

ROUGH EDGE

ROUGH BEAUTY

The Brotherhood Protectors

The Saving Series

SAVING LOVE

SAVING MAGNOLIA

SAVING LEATHER

Hot Hunks

Cove's Blind Date Blows Up

My Everyday Hero – Ledger

Tempting Tavor

Holiday Romances

A CHRISTMAS GETAWAY

<u>ALASKAN CHRISTMAS</u>

WHISPERS

CHRISTMAS IN THE SAND

CHRISTMAS IN JULY

Heroes & Heroines on the Field

TAKING A RISK

TEE TIME

The Twilight Crossing Series

THE BLIND DATE

www.ingramcontent.com/pod-product-compliance
Lightning Source LLC
Chambersburg PA
CBHW011442170626
46807CB00009B/3273